A LOVE MADE OUT OF NOTHING

ZOHARA'S JOURNEY

BARBARA HONIGMANN

A LOVE MADE OUT
OF NOTHING

ZOHARA'S JOURNEY

Two novels

Translated from the German

by John Barrett

VERBA MUNDI

David R. Godine · Publisher

BOSTON

First published in 2003 by
DAVID R. GODINE, PUBLISHER
Post Office Box 450
Jaffrey, New Hampshire 03452

LIBRARY OF CONGRESS CATALOGING-IN-PUBLICATION DATA
Honigmann, Barbara, 1949 –
[Liebe aus nichts. English]
A love made out of nothing ; Zohara's Journey : two novels
Barbara Honigmann ; translated from the German by John Barrett.
— 1st American ed.
p.   cm. — (Verba Mundi)
ISBN: 1-56792-187-6
I. Title: Love made out of nothing ; Zohara's journey. II. Honig-
mann, Barbara, 1949– Soharas Reise. English III. Barrett, John IV.
Title: Zohara's journey. V. Title. VI. Series.
PT2668.0495 L54   2002
833'.914   DC21

First edition, 2003
Printed in Canada

CONTENTS

A LOVE MADE OUT OF NOTHING

GINKGO BILOBA

This tree's leaf, entrusted
To my garden from the East,
Suggests some secret meaning
To enrich one who comprehends.

Is it *one* living being
That divides itself within?
Or are there *two* who choose
To be considered *one?*

The reply to such a query
Lies within this thought:
Do you not feel from my songs
That I am both *one* and paired?

J. W. von Goethe
The Book of Suleika

JUST AS HE'D ASKED to have it done in a letter he'd left for us — not really a will, just a letter, a few lines on a scrap of tablet paper — my father was buried in the traditional way in the Jewish Cemetery of Weimar. For decades, no one had been buried in that little cemetery on the way out of town, and my father's wish came as somewhat of a surprise, because during his entire life he'd had no ties to Judaism at all, not even a Hebrew name. The cantor, who had to be brought in from another city — a Jew from Saloniki who didn't know my father and had never even laid eyes on him — simply inserted his German name and, ridiculously, the title "Doctor" as well, into the proper places in the Hebrew chant, didn't omit a single one of the endless repetitions, and, with his Sephardic accent, garbled my father's name over and over again.

It was hard to believe that it was my father lying there in the coffin. I thought I just had to see him again, had to ask someone to open the coffin so I could see him again, but I didn't dare to because I was afraid to see him dead, just as I'd been afraid to see him sick, and I had to ask myself why I hadn't come sooner, hadn't at least tried. Maybe it would have been possible to get a visa earlier, but I hadn't even inquired about it, was afraid to, but perhaps there was a bit of vengefulness to it as well, because my father had deserted me, too, had deceived me, too. And why had he underlined the word "murder" in his letter?

After the funeral I went back up to Belvedere Palace, where my father had lived with his last wife. She was the directress of the Palace Museum, but in reality there was no such thing, because the restoration of Belvedere had never been completed and, in fact, had barely been started. Their apartment was under the roof, right next to the dumbwaiter that Goethe called "table-set-yourself" and had installed so that he and Karl August could picnic up there on the roof terrace. From the window you can see out over Belvedere Park, with the Ginkgo biloba tree that Goethe had imported and planted, and about which he wrote the famous poem. But the tree looks pretty scruffy and unimpressive and, on our walks through the park, my father and I had often asked ourselves whether it could really have been "this tree's leaf" in the famous poem, but that's what's written everywhere, and everyone around here always says it is.

I wanted to see my father's room again and take something to remember him by, but trying to pick something out was hard, and not the slightest bit comforting. His clothes were lying around the room just as forlornly as his body was right then, and even all those other objects that had been part of his life and contained some memory of it seemed merely like pieces that had fallen off, that had lost their connections and no longer had any meaning now; for a while they'd be pushed back and forth, held in my hand, but then soon be put away again, regardless. I picked up this or that, turned it and twisted it to see if maybe there wasn't something alive in there that I could coax out, like a small child does when he finds something new and shakes it and holds it up to his ear, then puts it into his mouth and bites it, because he doesn't know what to make of such an unfamiliar object and expects almost anything from it. But I realized that the memories had fallen out of those objects; now they'd be thrown out or given away and other people could start all over again and put their own stories into them. But the story of my father was over, was no longer connected with those things.

In a drawer I found a small notebook bound in red leather, an English pocket calendar from his emigré days, which I took for myself as well as the Russian wristwatch he always wore. It was a gift from Yefim Fraenkel, the German Literature specialist from Moscow with whom my father had worked at the Soviet News Agency in the Russian Zone in the first years after the war. After the Soviet News Agency was closed and Yefim Fraenkel had gone back to Moscow, he was exiled and sent to a camp, but my father only learned that the first time they met each other again twenty years later. Yefim Fraenkel visited him in Weimar and gave him the watch on that occasion and my father bought three pairs of jeans at Teen Fashions for Fraenkel's sons in Moscow.

Now the watch had stopped and couldn't be wound, so I took it in for repair right away, here in Paris. The watchmaker fixed it for me, but made derogatory remarks about Russian watches — they were solid enough, he said, but their works were crude and poorly finished. And then he asked me if I came from there and I answered, "No, no."

"Well, then, from where?"

"I'm not from there."

I'VE BEEN IN THIS CITY, Paris, for just a couple months, not even a whole year. I live in a basement apartment in the thirteenth arrondissement — I haven't been able to find anything better. From down here I look up at the street, at the feet of people walking by; in the beginning, just after I'd arrived, they were wearing sandals and going without stockings because it was hot outside — a very hot summer — but inside, in my apartment, it was cold and dark because the window only reaches a little above street level and hardly lets any light in, and I had to dress warmly, not to go out as is usually the case, but when I came in from the outside. I sat in my room as if I were in an observatory, with the city, which I couldn't see, revolving around me, and from my window I searched up and down the street as if I had a telescope, in order to see what was going to happen next.

Now, at least I have my furniture and things from Berlin. For the first few weeks there were just the bare walls and a folding bed that I'd borrowed and the everyday essentials — a set of cutlery, a plate, a hand towel, a glass, and a stool to sit on. Just like in prison, I thought then, not like a new world, and at night I had bad dreams about the cold and being exiled. Pretty soon, I wasn't so sure what I was really doing here. Yes, I'd wanted to break out of my old life and into a new one, out of a familiar language into a foreign one, and maybe I'd even hoped for some sort of transformation.

Hadn't I spent my whole life sighing, "To Paris, to Paris"? And then one day I was sitting in a train and the train was coming into a station and people were saying it was Paris. The loudspeakers were blaring it at me: "Pariii Est! Pariii Est!" And yes, I was coming from the east. I looked around the station, which is really big and bright, the way you do in a new apartment when you walk into it for the first time; you look at the bare walls and ask yourself what's waiting for you there and what sort of experiences you're going to have, and you're scared and curious at the same time and even proud that you've plunged into the adventure and now there's no going back anymore.

But as soon as I wanted to get out of the station and into the city, there was no sidewalk, no street there, only a rickety barrier, a construction site with bulldozers, cranes, noisy machines, and a gigantic excavation. I went back into the station again and out another exit, but there were the bulldozers, cranes, and noisy machines again and the gigantic, gaping excavation, and I frantically ran in and out of hundreds of entrances and exits again and it really seemed as if there were no access to the city. Then, suddenly, I was standing in a square directly in front of the station, with a boulevard leading away from it — a waterfall of a street, a broad river with brightly colored little ships, and I walked up and down both of its shores. But what next? I was feeling the slightest bit desperate, beginning to lose control — where, where am I going? Having arrived, I now had to go somewhere, but I'd never thought about the fact that I'd be coming into a big city with wide streets and avenues and districts spreading out in all directions, and that I'd have to decide where I was going to go, and it wouldn't just be a ball of dreams bouncing along in front of me that I'd run after and catch.

Every day I left my cave in the souterrain to go on expeditions across the length and breadth of the city, down streets, boulevards, and avenues, across tiny little squares and gigantic squares and through shady parks. And I sat down in churches and cafés along the way and took the Metro to the end of the line and walked miles through its passages and stairs and tunnels, and sometimes I got on a commuter train and rode back out of the city, and walked off into the flat landscape with a sort of élan, almost a frenzy, as if I could overrun the countryside and subjugate it.

And soon I'd seen a lot that I hadn't really wanted to see, and actually felt more like an immigrant to America a hundred years ago: there he is, sitting on Ellis Island, that damned island, cut off from a whole life behind him and he hasn't yet set foot in America and already senses the horrible truth about the New World and sometimes has to ask himself whether he hasn't given up too much for too little. But there's no going back to his Russian, Polish, Hungarian, Lithuanian, or whatever other kind of village; on the contrary, his brothers and sisters, aunts and uncles and friends want to follow right after him, by which time, he, the one who's still stagnating away there on Ellis Island, is supposed to have built something up — a new life.

Sometimes, in the middle of the city, in some street or other, I've simply gone into the entrance of a totally unfamiliar building and climbed up the steps as if I lived there and always just walked right in. There'd be a wide, stone stairway covered with soft carpet, so that your footsteps didn't make any noise, and I'd even stick my nose out of a rear window and see a secret garden, one without too much sun or too much shade, and suddenly I'd be struck by a completely unfamiliar smell, a foreign one, without any resemblance to anything I could recall, as if perhaps there really were a completely different world after all, where everything didn't remind you of everything else.

But when I went walking down streets and through courtyards and just wanted to look around a little to see what was there and what was going on, I didn't feel exactly welcome. People seemed suspicious, asked right away if I were looking for someone, and when I said, "No, no one, nothing, I'm just taking a walk," they acted like that was improper, out of order, and I'd disappear again through the nearest gate.

Once, right near my own street — which is so loud and full of traffic — I wandered into a neighborhood that's like a village in the middle of the city, a hilly, humpbacked quarter, with crooked streets that run up and down, around bends and curves, with little stairways, balconies, rusted lanterns, and old women in bathrobes and slippers who've probably been walking their dogs there for centuries. Every house is different from the next one, quite low — two stories at most — narrow, mostly crooked as well, leaning out over the street, making it seem even narrower. The streets all lead up to a tiny square on top of the hill. I looked around for a street sign and it said "Butte aux Cailles" — "Quail Hill." On top of Quail Hill — how could it be otherwise — cafés and taverns jostle against each other, chairs and tables are put out on the small sidewalks, almost between the cars, and there are swarms of people all over the place. It seemed to me as if some small nation were holding its yearly convention there — that's how much they all seemed to belong together. Now and then, drivers stopped beside the tables, cranked their windows down, and simply joined in the conversation. They all talk so much here, they just talk on and on.

I heard them, but I didn't understand them. They were greeting one another, kissing each other, laughing, going, coming, leaving again; then one of the men who'd just left appeared at a window of one of the houses across the way, opening it halfway out over the table. He yelled something else down and the others yelled something else up.

For a moment I wanted to sit down among them. I found a solitary empty chair at a table from which all the others had long since been taken away. But because it was so crowded I was still sitting right next to the people of Quail Hill. I was sitting there in the first row as if I were at a theater performance, right up against the stage, watching the drama of their national convention, and then I even recognized the structure of the play and how the roles were divided up. That is, the lead actors stayed seated the whole time and only the secondaries and extras had the entrances and exits. I had to laugh when they laughed, was already caught up in their play — then they looked at me questioningly. I understood. I'd taken a seat away from them. I'd been sitting there for half an hour already. So I left again and didn't know whether I should say goodbye as I was going or "Salut," couldn't bring myself to do it, and yet would like to have said, "See you again." As I walked away, I could still hear the sounds of the people of Quail Hill behind me for a long time.

Oh, it's wonderful to go strolling around on unfamiliar sidewalks, be a taker of walks, here, there, anywhere. But it's hard to come, stay a little while, and then leave again. And that I'd been one of them for a little while — they probably hadn't even noticed that.

On my expeditions, I constantly had to think about what I

was going to do here, whether I'd be able to make my way as an artist or whether I'd be able to find a job, and how. It turned out to be difficult to start my new life and I thought much more about everything that I'd left behind, about my father from whom I'd run away because he had demanded too much of me for my entire life, about the friends whom I'd gotten tired of, and about the Berliner Theater, where I didn't want to work any longer. Now I was writing postcards to my father, my friends, and my colleagues at the Berliner Theater and feeling far away and cut off, as detached and alone as Adam and Eve up there on the rampart of Notre Dame. Below them, hundreds of saints are lined up in a row, staring blankly; but those two, Adam and Eve, are standing up there alone — as if they want to jump — far apart from each other, no one beside them, and naked. And down below, at the foot of Notre Dame, it's teeming with people, whole nations are talking and calling out in many languages and running around in groups behind leaders with pennants. But some people are just standing there and looking up and some are talking and some are silent, some are strolling around, some are walking hurriedly, others are even running, some are arguing, some are kissing each other, some are sitting on benches, some are sleeping on the benches, some are reading, some are eating out of bags they've brought along or are buying themselves a Coca-Cola at a stand, and some are writing postcards, like I am.

Whenever I'd sit in a café, for hours at a time or even half a day, writing letters or reading a book I'd brought along, because in the beginning I only ever read books that had come from Berlin — in other words, ones I already knew — or whenever I'd study the vocabulary for the French course at the university extension and try to snap up the formulas for the everyday life around me — "Merci — merci de même" — I'd often be torn between the pleasant feeling of being abroad, of pride at having had the strength to separate myself from my old life, and a sort of homesickness that wasn't actually painful, but consisted merely of the fact that I was almost always thinking about some other time, an earlier one. For instance, the summers when I used to sit with my girlfriends in a café in Budapest, usually the Vörös- marty — which was actually called Gerbeaud's and dated from the Royal and Imperial days — among old ladies with a lot of jewelry around their necks and arms, among young writers eas- ily recognized by the heaps of paper that they wrote all over without looking up, and other young men who just absolutely had to be artists and with whom we were in love because of their paintings — which we hadn't seen, of course, but admired anyway. Hour after hour we'd sit there. Once we even set a nine hour record for uninterrupted sitting, talking, and eating cake. We ate a certain kind of small pastry called an "Indian," a light dough glazed with chocolate and filled with unsweetened whipped cream. We ate one Indian after another and didn't leave our seats — not to take a walk, not to go swimming in the Danube, not even to have a look at the city or the museums. We preferred to go on sitting together among the old ladies and the artists.

Back then we were unhappy because we felt an intense long- ing for something completely undefined; and now I was sitting here, still longing for something completely undefined, home- sick for my girlfriends and my father. Sitting here as if I were on Ellis Island, an immigrant, an emigrant, a taker of walks.

WHEN THE TRUCK parked outside my souterrain, with its double wheels directly in front of the half of the window that extended above ground, I knew right away it was bringing me the things from Berlin that I'd packed up and carefully tied closed and labeled, day after day, piece by piece. I'd packed them into a container, a great, big metal box — something like what used to be called a "steamer trunk" — which they'd plunked down in the middle of my room. But now everything was all jumbled up inside the container — boxes and cartons gaped wide open, things that had been underneath now lay on top, tapes and string hung down without rhyme or reason and were tangled into knots that couldn't be undone, some things that I was sure I'd packed were nowhere to be found, and a few things had been added that didn't even belong to me and hadn't been there to start with. And in between were packages that still bore the dust from the cellar of my old apartment, packages that I'd never opened but just dragged along through the years.

I've started to move things out of the container and into the apartment — a few pieces of furniture, the books, the cartons, the easel, my pictures, and the dishes; and, after the first few trips to the store, groceries in unfamiliar packages and all sorts of new things — the first butter, first sugar, first light bulbs — got mixed in with the old things. And the plugs all had to be changed.

In among the cartons all the way at the bottom is where I'd stuck the letters, all those old letters that I'd bundled up and saved over the years, with pages that were getting yellower and yellower. I hadn't unfolded them for years and even now I couldn't bring myself to look at them as I stacked them up and bundled them together and put them back in the cartons at the bottom again. If I did happen to glance at one of them, I got scared, because those pages from another time were so distant from me that they seemed like messages from the underworld that could pull me right down into it, if I looked at them too long.

On top of one of the bundles at the very bottom of a carton is where I'd put the letter my father had written to me right after my departure:

> *My dear Daughter,*
>
> *I have to tell you that I really can't understand all of this, even though we've often talked about your leaving.*
>
> *I think again and again about a Hölderlin verse that has never left my head since my boyhood years at the Odenwald School, so long, long ago:*
> *"We wanted to part, held it to be good and proper.*
> *"When we did, why did the deed frighten us like a* murder?
> *"Oh, we know ourselves so little."*
>
>

With love,
Your father
>

"Murder" had been underlined by my father.

As a child I was a little child and as an adult I remained a little adult. My father was never satisfied with my figure, maybe even unhappy about it; he never stopped making derogatory remarks about the way I looked, and because my appearance never seemed to please him, I had difficulty adjusting to it myself. He told me he loved me anyway, but he said it in a way that was reproachful, as if I'd never returned his love. He accused me of not loving him enough, even of coldness and indifference; our conversations were always too short, not extensive enough, I wasn't paying proper attention to him, was distracted, called much too infrequently — and yet he was the one who'd gone away. And so, because we always lived apart from one another and because of those reciprocal demands that could never be fulfilled, our love remained a love at a distance, as if it were only a collection of encounters and common experiences and never a togetherness.

My father was married four times, to my mother somewhere in the middle of it all — she was his second wife. I can no longer remember when they lived together, only the times when I visited my father on weekends and during vacations, in the apartments of his third and fourth wives — my mother's successors. They were the apartments of strangers, where it was hard for me to recognize that it was my father's place and where the few things that I brought along, or was given, and which accumulated over the years, were stored in a cardboard box. After the weekend, when I went back to my mother, the box was put away again.

Saturdays, my father always picked me up at school with the car, and the whole morning I'd be afraid that I'd have to stay late because I did something stupid or absent-minded and he'd have to stand and wait in front of school for an hour and would scold me when I finally came — a bad start for our weekend. We had to drive all the way across the city to his apartment. That was like a trip to another country, because otherwise I just spent my time in the neighborhood around my mother's house in a quiet outlying district, where you could roller-skate in the street and run through the gardens to the Spree River. My father lived in an entirely different part of the city, right in the center, where I didn't know anyone and had no girlfriends. A house-keeper served us lunch; my father's third wife, an actress who was much younger than he, usually only came home in the afternoon after rehearsal. She had a big vanity in her room and a gigantic wardrobe from which I was sometimes allowed to take clothing to play "dress up." Once, when my father was taking his afternoon nap, I sat down at the vanity and made myself up, with black eyebrows and lashes, green and violet and blue around my eyes, pink on my cheeks, and red on my lips, and I took a slip with red dots and a hat from the actress's closet and put them on. Then I awakened my father. He looked at me without knowing what to make of it and then immediately wiped everything off again with his hand, without even looking.

In the evenings we often accompanied the actress to the the-ater, and my father and I would stand in the wings beside the fireman and watch the play in which she was appearing. We pre-ferred that spot next to the fireman to sitting in the audience, because the illusion was not as overpowering there; the play was going on in only one room of that big building, the other rooms of which were still visible to us, and the coming and going of people beside and behind us and around the stage was reassuring and dizzying at the same time. When stage hands or actors on their way to the canteen pushed open the big door through which the sets were brought in and out — the big door that led into the courtyard — then the evening sky, often still light in the

summer, would be visible as well as the courtyards of the neighboring buildings and even the canteen itself, a small pavilion.
The sounds of the city and the courtyards and the loud conversations from the canteen would carry over to us and almost into
the gripping atmosphere of the performance and the darkness in
which the spectators were sitting motionless, following the play;
only the two of us would be standing there between the darkened auditorium and the artificial world on stage and the world
outside behind the big door — which, somehow or other, still
didn't seem to be the real world, either. The stagehands, each
with a bottle of beer in his jacket pocket, would already be
erecting new sets on a section of the stage that was dark and
concealed from the spectators but not from us, while the actors
waiting to go on were sitting around beside the stage, reading
the evening paper. Sometimes, already halfway on stage, they'd
wave or make a quick face at us. When the performance was
over, we'd go into the actress's dressing room and I'd watch
while she wiped off her makeup and took off her costume and
transformed herself into my father's wife, my mother's successor.

My father even wanted to have a child by the actress, but
somehow they were never able to manage it and several times
during weekends with my father I visited her in a hospital where
she'd been admitted because of a miscarriage or a tubal pregnancy, and we had to watch while she cried. Sometimes I
brought along my toe shoes and tutu from my ballet lesson and,
to cheer her up, danced a solo or the pas de deux from *Swan
Lake* or *Sleeping Beauty* in between the beds and around the
bedside tables on wheels, with the aluminum bedposts for my
partners. I whistled the music or sang along *la-la-la*. And once
they took me along into the doctor's office and showed me a
glass in which an embryo was swimming in some fluid and said
it was my brother, who'd never be born.

Later, my father left the actress and married an even younger woman, the museum directress from Weimar, and moved into Belvedere Palace with her. She was his fourth and last wife. By that time, he'd already had enough of Berlin and it probably suited him to retire to the Belvedere attic, next to Goethe and Karl August's "table-set-yourself," rather far away from everything else. They lived completely alone in the palace, which remained under construction throughout all those years.

From then on, I really did have to travel to another city to see my father. Sometimes we met halfway or went off together for a few days, to a hotel in Prague or Budapest or somewhere in the mountains. Later, when I had an apartment by myself, he even came back to Berlin and slept on my sofa in the kitchen and behaved just like a visitor, as if he'd never lived in that city.

During my entire childhood, I commuted back and forth between my parents and it hurt me to come and go, to come back again and leave again, and so there was probably never anything like real familiarity between us, because, over and over again, each time we said goodbye a shell of estrangement settled over everything.

My mother came from Bulgaria. She'd met my father in England and, after the war, followed him to Berlin, because they wanted to build a new Germany. But she could never adjust to Berlin. She always felt a great deal of hostility toward that city where she was always going in the wrong direction and getting lost and could never orient herself at all, and even after many years she still spoke German poorly and with a strong accent, so that everyone asked her where she came from. And because she'd already lived for many years in Vienna, Paris, and London, she couldn't just say "I'm from Bulgaria." But no one really wanted to hear the whole story. So she decided one day — long after my father had left her and she'd been alone all the time

— to return to Bulgaria. In Sofia she still had family and friends from before the war and she hoped she'd be able to get her bearings better there and finally be able to return to her native language. She postponed her decision for a long time, but after I was done with school and going to the university, she went to Sofia and found herself an apartment and never once came back to Berlin.

During vacations, I often visited my mother in Bulgaria and we traveled together to the Black Sea or the Rila Mountains. But as the years passed, she tended more and more to speak only Bulgarian, a language that I didn't think was very pretty and which I didn't understand, so that I sat there like a stranger among the uncles and aunts and friends from before the war. Shortly before her death, we couldn't even talk to one another any longer, because all she understood was Bulgarian, which I'd never really learned.

ON THE MAP OF PARIS, which served as the first picture I put up on the wall of my souterrain, I immediately started to look for the streets where my parents had lived before the war — I even circled them with a red pencil, although I wasn't at all sure whether I should go there. What could I expect to see? Besides, I didn't want to follow my parents' footsteps forever, even if I knew that I'd never get away from them and that my emigration was perhaps just a dream of real separation, the wish for a rootless life. Perhaps more than anything else, I've been running away from my parents and yet still go on trotting along behind them.

When they were living in Paris, my parents didn't know each other yet; my father was married to another woman and my mother to another man. She'd come from Vienna as a refugee and my father was a correspondent for a paper, the *Vossische Zeitung*, before he, too, became a refugee.

My mother said she'd been rich in those days and had an apartment on the Quai d'Orsay with a view of the Seine — an apartment with huge rooms, halls, and a whole semicircle of windows — and knew the entire Parisian art world, "tout Paris," all the people who'd moved to Paris from every conceivable country, and she'd entertained lavishly and danced all night in a low-cut pink silk dress, a hat, and a feather boa. In the cellar of our Berlin apartment, I did, in fact, find an old pasteboard box with a feather boa and a pink satin handbag that had probably matched her gown. My girlfriends played dress up with it and I had a hard time really believing that those stage props had once played a part in my mother's life.

Some time or other, I walked along the Quai d'Orsay and stopped in front of her building — I just picked one out, because I didn't actually know which one it had been. Naturally there's nothing at all to see there; on the contrary, it's as if a wave had broken over her presence and simply washed everything away.

When Hitler followed my mother to Paris, she moved to London. There, she married my father, who'd become a journalist for Reuters in the meantime because there no longer was a *Vossische Zeitung*. He'd separated from his first wife and my mother from her first husband. Hitler didn't come to London, but he did make it rain bombs on the city every night, so that they kept having to find new apartments, because the old ones were bombed to pieces. As it was, the only place they'd sleep was in a windowless bathroom, because, if you did manage to survive, the biggest risk was from the splinters of shattering window panes. During the day, my father put together war reports for the English newspapers at Reuters, while my mother worked in a defense plant, helping put together English submarines for the war against Germany. They wanted to fight back. And Hitler was beaten. He lost and my parents won. They left England again and went back to where it had all begun, to the place where Hitler had started to chase them, to Berlin.

My father got there first, with a few suitcases, after a roundabout journey through half of Europe, for although the war was indeed over, things still weren't like they were in peacetime. During the trip, he'd made the decision not to work for Reuters and the English any longer, but to desert to the Russians in East Berlin. He'd become a Communist.

My mother came almost a year later, as if she'd been hesitating. From London, she'd gone first to Bulgaria in order to look for her family and friends and show them that she herself was still alive, and only then did she meet up with my father again in Berlin. She arrived wearing blood-red fingernail polish, to hear him tell it.

Because they were Jews, the emigration and the bombing of London weren't the worst of it. My parents could even say they'd been lucky; but for the rest of their lives, they had to live with the pictures and reports about those who hadn't been lucky and that must have been a heavy burden — so heavy that they always acted as if they hadn't had anything to do with all that and as if they hadn't had any relatives who died in a ghetto or were gassed at Auschwitz. My father much preferred just talking about his ancestors on the Bergstrasse in Hesse, who'd been the court physicians and court bankers of the grand dukes of Hesse-Darmstadt. And in the end, they'd come to Berlin to build a new Germany, one which was to be entirely different from the old one, and, for that reason, it would be better not to talk about the Jews at all anymore. But somehow things didn't work out and the day came when they even had to justify their choice of the country where they'd spent their exile — why was it a Western country and not the Soviet Union? My mother at least thought she knew why she felt worse and worse: she'd already spent too much time moving from one country to another, and now she wanted to go home again. But my father had actually come home, to Germany, the country he'd come from — even if it wasn't to Hesse-Darmstadt but to East Berlin, to the Russians, the Communists. Maybe it was that act of desertion that made it still seem like a foreign country when he thought about his origins. At any time at all, no matter what the occasion, I'd hear him say, "Actually I don't know where I'm from and don't even know where I belong now." And once he added, "Perhaps everything has always been like it was with Martha." When I asked him who Martha was and what she had to do with anything and what had happened to her, he said, "It's an old story, from my childhood, but it probably never came to an end. All of my ideas, my professions, my wives, and even the places where I've lived my lives, everything was really just Martha the whole time."

We were in the process of carrying full shopping bags up the road from Oberweimar to Belvedere Palace. Almost every day my father walked down to do his shopping at the little state-run store, just for whatever they needed — bread, milk, butter, eggs, beer — and the sales ladies always addressed him as "Herr Professor," although he'd already explained to them a thousand times that he wasn't a professor and never had been. We'd put the bags down and were taking a rest at the crossroads, where you can choose between two routes — the broad Belvedere Avenue, where you walk along in the shade of the old trees on both sides, or the back way across the Ilm meadows and fields, on a path that becomes fairly steep toward the end and isn't very good for climbing up with full shopping bags. But from there you have a clear view of the entire region, even over to Buchenwald.

"When I was a little boy," my father told me, "I once wanted to write and perform a play. I was absolutely taken with the idea and announced it to my parents; it would be called *Martha* and they were to invite the whole family to the premiere on a certain day. My father, who was a professor, was proud of me and invited the whole family and his colleagues from the sanatorium to our grandiose apartment in a large villa in Wiesbaden, and I got busy preparing for the big evening, cutting out costumes, transforming the living room into a passable stage setting, writing the program notes, composing a list of the characters, and even sending selected people extra announcements and invitations to the premiere of *Martha*. But when it came to the point where the uncles and aunts and colleagues from the sanatorium had gathered in the theater/living room and were waiting for *Martha* to begin — in other words, when the grand moment I'd been preparing for so long had finally come — it suddenly struck me that I'd forgotten just one thing in my great excitement and joy: namely, to write the play. *Martha* had only been my dream of a play, the dream of a grand evening that was to be mine alone, my success and my fame, but the play didn't exist at all; I had completely forgotten to write it. Despite that, I appeared on stage and said:

"'This is frightful.

"'This is dreadful.

"'This is absolutely awful.'

"And that was all there was of *Martha*."

SOMETIMES IT SEEMED almost impossible for me to impose any sort of order on all those mixed-up pieces of my life's work that had come tumbling out of the container at me, and I was already exhausted by my impressions of my new world. I really no longer even had the strength to get up and get going, and felt much more like just staying in bed to catch my breath, and I often thought that I'd had just about enough of big changes and that I'd better call a halt to this perpetual motion, because I was already winded.

Why had I left everything lying around behind me like someone who'd had to run away?

It had been just one of those ideas — that you always had to go off to a new country, a new home, even if it were only some other province. In the entire city of Berlin, nothing was ever talked about other than the fact that you couldn't stay in one spot forever; it would be a childish life, you'd be like someone who never went out of the house. That's all they ever talked about anywhere, in the canteen of the Berliner Theater or in my apartment when we were sitting around the big table in the kitchen. Really, we hardly got out of our apartments at all in those days — what was the point, everything was so familiar that we were sick of it. Inside, in our apartments, we moped around and fantasized about everything that was "out there" and had difficulty imagining the reality of another life and of other cities and countries, and wondered whether things would be the same there or completely different and how people got along. We played loud music into the night — Bob Dylan or Bach cantatas — until the neighbors came and asked if we'd gone crazy and if maybe we didn't have to go to work the next morning.

I had a little apartment in the northern part of Berlin, one room in which the washing machine stood next to my desk and where I could never get a telephone. In front of the building was the stop for the number 57 bus, which I took for years and years, first to the university and then to the Berliner Theater. It was the same theater where, as a child, I'd stood in the wings with my father and watched his third wife, the actress. In the meantime, I'd become a dramaturge and had to write short articles for the program notes, run to the library to look up material about the staging, or compose notes for the rehearsals, which I'd show to the dramaturges who'd been working there for decades and whose assistant I was. Then sometime or other they threw me out of the theater; that is to say, the temporary contract I'd had for years simply wasn't renewed — a contract that I should have complained about to the Fair Employment Office a long time ago, but since things had somehow managed to go on right up until that day, I'd been too lazy to get upset about the injustice. And I was also slowly getting fed up with always taking the bus from in front of my building to the Berliner Theater and I'd even argued with my friends about whether we hadn't just had enough of friendships that had lasted too long and this eternal sitting around at each other's places. Familiar things had become familiar to the point of boredom, so that exhaustion and weakness were spreading all through me — and a laziness about life that scared me.

Once, after the premiere of *Egmont*, I and all the others received bouquets of roses from the director. We'd celebrated the whole night, into the early hours of the morning, and then I'd walked home through the gray dawn; it was June, the beginning of summer, you didn't have to worry about being chilly. I'd left the casement window open in my room and both sides were cranked out. The main streetcar terminal extended back from below my window, the first trolleys were just creeping out of the sheds; behind lay the central slaughterhouse, from which the acrid, nauseating stench of animals constantly drifted over. Next to the commuter station on Lenin Avenue, the Werner Seelenbinder Hall was announcing yet another party anniversary, and behind it, the factory buildings and chimneys stretched off toward the horizon and in between rose a small, pale blue church tower. As I came in from celebrating the premiere, the sun was just rising over it all, turning the blackish gray of the waning night into the yellowish and reddish grays of the morning and I stood there with the bouquet in my hand, looking at that landscape that was like a troubled and threatening sea — the streetcars and sheds and the animals trucked in for slaughter squealing behind bars and the chimneys, with the morning sun flooding over it all. There were already a lot of bouquets in my room. I dried every one I'd ever been given and put them all around on the shelves and chests, so that a dust-covered, *forest primeval* of flowers or a flower cemetery had grown up and, for a considerable period of time, had been filling the landscape of my room with rank overgrowth. That particular morning, however, after the premiere of *Egmont*, at the sight of the wide open window, I didn't want to dry and save flowers anymore. I threw the bunch of roses out of the window in a high arc — they landed somewhere on the streetcar terminal. Then I cut down the *forest primeval* and cleaned out the cemetery on my shelves and chests, and tossed out all the other dried flower bouquets just the way I did the first bunch.

Occasionally, one of the actors at the Berliner Theater would recite a Rilke verse while we were sitting in the canteen:

> . . . and go away? Where? Into uncertainty
> far away, to an alien warm country
> that will matter as little as
> the set behind the action — garden or wall;
> and go away? Why? From impulse, inclination,
> from impatience, dim expectation,
> incomprehensibility, unreasonableness.

Then we'd argue about Rilke, whom some idolized and others just couldn't stand, and about the uncertain foreign country, the lack of understanding, the incomprehensibility of things — and it was half serious and half just talk and usually stopped when someone yelled, "OK, that's enough of that!" However, when someone from the group really did up and leave to find a new territory, that new country, they all got very upset and he was condemned by those who'd stayed behind, as if he'd betrayed them.

The first one they talked about that way was Alfried. He was a director and was one of the first who left the theater and the country. They accused him of being frivolous and thought he probably had no idea of the price he'd have to pay. And all the others who followed him were accused the same way; and I listened and knew that some day it would be my turn.

At home, in my room, I sat among the dried flowers, stared out of the window at the streetcar terminal and the stockyards, and could hardly believe that Alfried had simply torn himself loose from everything. I started to write him long letters, meter-long communiqués about my life and my love for him, which had now turned into those pieces of paper. The letters piled up on the desk because I had no idea where he was and where I should be sending them. So they just lay around and, in the end, I threw the meter-long, piled-up letters into the dumpster, where everything you throw in falls so far down that you can't find it or get it out again.

Alfried sometimes waited for me after a performance and we'd go for something to eat or walk through Friedrichshain, first up "Rubble Mountain" and then around the little lake, or on Sundays we'd take a trip to another city. And we always wrote each other letters, actually little notes that we'd shove under each other's door — not like other people, when no one was there, but right when the other person was at home, because that's the way we concealed ourselves from each other. We never said, "I love you," and never "I love you, too." We just gestured and gestures can always be interpreted any way you want them to be. But above all, not a word. An unintelligible pantomime.

Whenever Alfried did visit me, it was late at night. The door to the building would have been locked long before and he'd have to stand in the courtyard and yell my name, because there was no bell by the door, and then I'd run down the stairs and let him in. He'd only stay a few hours and leave before dawn, so that, come morning, nobody saw whoever it was who'd been doing the loud yelling at night, and I myself was no longer so sure that even I'd seen him. The next day we were colleagues at the Berliner Theater again.

Alfried had told me that he didn't want to have me come to

31

his apartment, but never told me the reason why. He didn't say a thing and I didn't ask — we remained silent about it, the way we did about everything else. But I couldn't understand, and, as a sort of revenge, I planned to simply break into his apartment some day to see what there was that he had to hide. He'd said something about where the key was hidden. I remembered, and when he'd gone away for a few days, I decided to go over and take the key from its hiding place and open the door, and even took other keys with me to help me break in. I wanted to get into everything in his apartment, rummage through his drawers, pull things out, throw them around, and leave a note saying "I WAS HERE," in order to shatter the layer of silence, or, even better, sit down in the middle of the mess I'd made by pulling everything out and throwing it on the floor and wait until he came back and found me. What would he have said then?

I didn't find the place where the key was hidden, even though I felt around and scratched and thumped on the walls and the window sills and the window frames beside the door, centimeter by centimeter, all to no avail. But when I randomly picked out one of the keys I'd brought along and tried it in the lock, the door opened quite easily — it sprang open in front of me and I was suddenly standing in Alfried's apartment. I walked through his rooms, saw where he worked, where he slept, his kitchen with the little balcony in front of the window, the dirty dishes he hadn't washed before he left — I saw it all, but couldn't touch a thing, didn't even want to look around anymore. I didn't feel any closer to him for having broken in amongst all his things, but, instead, much more distant than before. I didn't stay there, didn't pull anything out, didn't write a note saying "I WAS HERE," but left everything untouched and locked the door behind me again with the wrong key, so that everything was left exactly as it had been.

From the very beginning I hated Alfried's name; I could hardly bring myself to say it because it sounded so Germanic and because I didn't want to love a German, because I couldn't and wouldn't forgive the Germans for what they had done to the Jews. Because the Germans had been murderers, I couldn't say Alfried's name and called him "dearest" or "my love." Because I did love him, almost against my will, and that love often seemed like a connection or even an adhesion that we couldn't pull away from.

Sometimes I wished or was afraid we'd have a child. But I saw the child in nightmares, the way it was put together loosely from individual pieces and then came undone and fell apart and couldn't stand upright. I didn't tell Alfried a thing about those dreams because I knew he wouldn't want to hear anything about them. He avoided any mention of where we came from, our similarities or dissimilarities, he didn't want to see the reality of that life of mine — which I hadn't chosen, but which still weighed heavily on me and whose inner truth was simultaneously obvious and hidden, even for me. Perhaps he'd had a difficult past, too, but we kept quiet about everything, as if there were nothing there. One hint was already too much, every question an imposition. Perhaps it was fear of a misunderstanding or the inability to recognize the other person. And there was even something of a rivalry between us. It was always a matter of a winner and a loser, and yet we didn't compete for victory, but for defeat — we each felt we'd lost and accused the other one of being the winner. The less we talked about things, the more clearly they came out. At the same time, we'd never look directly at each other, just sneak an ashamed glance from the side or from a distance, never right in the face, as if by light of day we were afraid, after a terrible night or some bloody sacrifice.

After he'd gone away, Alfried sent me picture postcards from every imaginable city in Europe — never a letter — and I never found his address on any of the cards. In the canteen of the Berliner Theater, people told what they'd heard about his productions in other cities, this or that play, here or there — in Hamburg, in Frankfurt, in Munich; and occasionally someone brought in a newspaper article by one of the critics and passed it around.

And I'd sit around in my apartment in the midst of the flower cemetery, not feeling at all happy in my own skin anymore and thinking that leaving could even be something like a metamorphosis, during which you'd simply shed the old skin. I wanted to emigrate, preferably to Paris, to learn a new language and take up something entirely new, perhaps get even farther away, to America for example, where no one I knew had ever been. I'd really be the first one to arrive there; no one would know me and no one would ask me questions, but if they did, I could answer anything at all, something I'd thought up from an entirely different life, and everything would start all over again from the very beginning.

I wanted to tear myself loose from that nest of nothing but familiar people, countryside, and political conditions, from the language and the certainty that I found in it all and which I knew I'd perhaps never find again.

For a few more months I mulled things over, but then I just walked in and filled out the application that was required, in a building that I could find easily, because it was the same one in which I'd been applying for a phone for years without success and where I'd gotten the cards for the delivery of wood and coal for the stove that stood beside the washing machine and the desk.

In no time at all there was a white card sitting in my mailbox that was the signal for the exodus and the beginning of proceedings, at the end of which you'd be told that you could go now, just as you'd wished, and that there was only a short interval during which you were permitted to stay; before the interval expired, you had to be gone. They brought the container to my room and everything I wanted to take along disappeared into it. Not much would fit and I had to look at everything from the standpoint of its usefulness and its history, and I mainly picked out things I couldn't part with — photos, pictures, books, letters, a few manuscripts of plays, the easel, some household items, a couple of tools, and clothes for different seasons.

Then I had to say goodbye to my friends and, in the act of leaving, was reconciled with them and even with my colleagues from the Berliner Theater, and it was like a painful wrenching or an amputation when I said that the story was over now and I didn't know what its sequel would be. In the final days I cried a lot, as soon as I got up in the morning, because I'd cried myself to sleep the night before. But one morning I walked out of the apartment, locked it up, and didn't put the key into my pocket as usual, but took it to the district housing authority instead and turned it in there. Then I no longer had an apartment to go back to — it had been locked behind me once and for all and I was outside. In order to fix in my mind the moment I left, I looked at my watch. It was nine o'clock in the morning, just like it was nine o'clock in the morning every day. My neighbor was going shopping, just the way she went shopping every day and she even told me she'd heard that the first tomatoes were finally in at the market   six marks fifty a kilo, a ripoff.

DURING THE FIRST weeks in Paris, I was often afraid of going under. Lots of people gave me good advice — friends of friends, whose addresses they'd written down in my notebook, or friends from before, who'd left long ahead of me and then ended up here. But mostly they'd adapted quite well to their new surroundings and were so involved in their new lives that I had trouble recognizing them again. They said they wanted to help me, I should call again or drop in again, some other time, later, and they gave me addresses and more new names, and when we'd discussed everything, we often just sat there or went off somewhere else, had something to drink, told about our adventures since we'd left, and asked each other endlessly — as if it were a litany — do you know him and do you know her or him?

The names and addresses they gave me — a big, long list that got longer and longer because they kept giving me more and more names and addresses of theaters, publishers, bookstores, little magazines, and actors' agents — I looked them all up to ask about a job. Honestly, I really didn't want that kind of work anymore, because I knew I'd end up being merely an assistant again, which I'd been much too long already at the Berliner Theater, and that was not going to go on for the rest of my life.

So one day I quit trying to find something at theaters, publishers, bookstores, little magazines, and actors' agents, and struck out on an entirely different path. I went to the Ecole des Beaux Arts, applied for a scholarship, and registered right away for some painting courses — studies from nature and drawing from a model. Instead of letting the wave of this new life simply roll over me, exhaust me, or even drag me to the bottom, I wanted to use its movement to change places for myself.

I'd brought my easel along from Berlin. It's just a light portable one, specially designed for carrying around and putting up out in the open, but it was always standing around in my apartment and often fell over when I painted on it, mostly at night — self-portraits, as if I wanted to reassure myself that I was still there, portraits of Alfried, in order to be closer to him since he was always concealing himself, the view from my window toward the streetcar terminal, the central stockyards, and the small grayish church tower on the horizon, and portraits of the authors of books I loved, in order to respond to them, to pay homage. Painting was a kind of holding on to things whose proximity was wavering and uncertain, like the very easel on which I painted the pictures. It came from my friend Blanca, who'd inherited it from her father, an exiled Spanish painter. When Franco finally died, he went running back to Spain head over heels, leaving his easel standing here — which Blanca passed on to me before she herself moved to England. The exile was over, but she'd never gotten to know Spain except from the legends her parents told her, and she was afraid people there would mistakenly call her a

German, just as people in Germany had mistakenly called her a Spaniard for years. Now that she could finally choose, she wanted to choose another country — a third one, a neutral one — to live in.

I sometimes take the easel and fold it up so that it looks like a little suitcase, tie the paints and the brushes on top wrapped in a cloth, and go out to paint a view of the city. Most of the time I never really finish, because I can't figure out how to limit it to one section. Then I go back to my souterrain and paint the things that are lying on the table — leftovers from breakfast, for example, or pictures from photographs that I pull out of my boxes, or the view from my window, which, because it only reaches halfway above street level, shows me a defined section of the city, so that I'm not put off by its endlessness.

The first person I saw here regularly was Marc, who called himself Jean-Marc in Paris. He was an American from New York, but his parents were Jews from Riga. They called him up every week and he didn't have the nerve to tell them that was too often for him. He'd almost gotten his architecture degree, but he still came to the nature studies at the Ecole des Beaux Arts. We sat together there and took the Metro home together, or walked — although it was a long way — and looked for open squares and nice views that we could plan on drawing later. Jean-Marc knew the city much better and noticed things more, perhaps because he was studying architecture and looked at buildings the same way he looked at people.

He lived under a mansard roof, not far from me; I climbed up there to visit him, or he came down to my place in the basement. Sundays he worked in the laundromat near the Place d'Italie and I kept him company now and then, got something to drink or some fruit at the grocery on the corner that's always open, even Sundays and late at night. In the short time that I've been here, it's changed owners three times. First they were Turks, then Arabs, and now they're all blacks and the whole family is always standing around in the store.

There wasn't much for Jean-Marc to do at the laundromat, and we could read and talk; sometimes I even took my sketch book and pencils along, or pens and India ink, and we drew each other. We spoke French to each other. That was a compromise so that neither of us would have the advantage of speaking his or her native language. Mostly we talked about our backgrounds, about our parents, where they came from, and how they'd fled from the Nazis. The routes of their emigration and their experiences in those foreign countries were like myths of our childhood days and of our lives in general — like the wanderings of Ulysses, legends told a thousand times. Now we repeated them for each other, sang them, almost, in a chorus, like different verses of one and the same song.

Jean-Marc talked about New York and I told him about Bulgaria, Weimar, and my life in Berlin. Jean-Marc corrected me: I should say "East Berlin," but I explained to him that for us there was only one Berlin. There weren't two sides, there was just the one city where we lived, and then there was West Berlin, but that wasn't like another part that belonged with our part, it was something over on the other side. That he couldn't understand.  And there was something else he couldn't understand, that he criticized me for, over and over again: how Jews could bring themselves to live in Germany after all that had happened to them there. He would never set foot in that country. And when I once mentioned how much I'd like to show him Berlin and Weimar, Belvedere Palace and the Ginkgo biloba, he said no, that wouldn't interest him at all. Even in his high school days, he'd done everything to avoid studying German and took Greek and Latin instead because there was no other choice. I said that it happened to be my native language and what he was talking about amounted to a ban on it. "Yes," he said, "a ban." That's what he meant, a ban like the one pronounced against Spain. They drove out the Jews, who never returned, and that's why the golden age faded in Spain. We argued about whether that was right or not. We didn't argue — like we did in Berlin — about the place you wanted to live, or could live, but whether you would permit yourself to live in one place or the other. It was hard for me to explain what reasons my parents had for going to Berlin and now I was arguing with Jean-Marc like I used to with Alfried and we were criticizing each other for things that were entirely external to us. Just as much as Alfried had withdrawn himself from me back then, Jean-Marc was now trying to pull me entirely over to his side, and it was tempting to simply let myself be drawn over into his world. He tried to convince me to go to New York with him, said he knew that's what I wanted, but, though I knew he was right, I couldn't go that far. He told me that if I wanted to emigrate, he'd marry me and then everything would be quite simple, I'd get off Ellis Island quickly. But I said, "No, no, once I'm on Ellis Island, I'll never get off again. Ellis Island is my home." "Ah," said Jean-Marc, "there's no such thing as Ellis Island anymore."

IN MY BROWN HANDBAG, which has a stuck zipper and is completely stretched out of shape because I cram books and sketch pads into it, is my father's letter, which I still carry around with me, the one he left for me in Frankfurt, the first stopover after I left. I didn't put it in the bottom of the box with the other letters, but crumpled it up as soon as I'd read it, then smoothed it out again later, folded it up, and stuck it into my handbag along with the envelope. And there it sits, in with my new passport and identity cards and Metro tickets, cosmetics, perfume, and the keys to the souterrain — cut off, exiled.

After I'd packed the container and turned in the key in Berlin, I also had to buy a ticket and name the place where I was going, and even at the office where I formally declared the end of my life in Berlin, they wanted to hear the name of a town — a destination; they couldn't have cared less if I'd said "X" or "Y," but I had to say something and because I couldn't bring myself to say Paris or America and because my father happened to be there, back in his home town for the first time, and because, in addition, my play was being performed there and perhaps because it wasn't really going somewhere but was rather a kind of returning since my ancestors had come from the Hessian Bergstrasse that my father had always talked about so proudly, I said, "Frankfurt. Single ticket to Frankfurt am Main. One way."

I'd hoped that my father would be standing there to meet me as the train pulled into the main station at Frankfurt, because I'd sent him a telegram saying, "Arrive Thursday 18:46 Frankfurt Hauptbahnhof." But I didn't see him when I got off the train and couldn't find him as I ran back and forth on the platform calling his name like an idiot because I thought I saw him here or there, in among the crowd. He hadn't come — just left me a letter at the theater.

Since there was no one else in the city I knew, I went to visit the director who was putting on my play and who'd invited me to come see it. I told him how I'd showed the play to the dramaturges who'd been at the Berliner Theater for years and how they'd just refused it with a wave of the hand, "No, that won't work, no." And the director said, "Well, we'll see." Then I told him that I didn't want to go back to Berlin and the Berliner Theater, but wanted to move to Paris or even farther away, and he answered, "Ach, we all dream about moving away and getting out, but that's really just an illusion, you could end up being very lonely and losing everything, so most of the time you just stay where you are." And he asked me if I weren't sort of afraid of being in a strange place and I said, "That's exactly what I'm looking for, adventure and a hiding place."

He took me along with him to the theater that was located on the outskirts of the city. We went there by streetcar. Then we walked across a rear courtyard, climbed a flight of stairs, and were standing in a wide foyer with a few tables and chairs where the actors were sitting and drinking coffee or beer. There was still a lot of time left until the beginning of the performance. The director introduced me to the actors, told me their names and which roles they'd be playing and we said hello to each other. The leading lady was the only one who failed to return my greeting when we went over to her table; she didn't offer to shake hands, but turned away in an almost hostile way, and even started to cry and said the performances were awful because there was almost no audience, as I'd soon see, and it was nerve-wracking and senseless to play to an empty house with no one looking at her — sheer torture for an actress. Besides, all you had to do was read the newspapers to know what a flop it was. She was ashamed, upset first thing in the morning and all day long, knowing that every evening she had to come to this damned theater that no one knew or cared about. A director who didn't have a clue and a ridiculous play — it hadn't been worth the trouble, the week-long rehearsals, all that work. It had all been a waste of time, not worth a thing, not a thing. So awful. Awful.

She wouldn't stop crying, just went on and on. I couldn't even see her face because, as she went on crying, she turned around toward the back of her chair and put her head on her arms. All I could see was her hair, her neck, and the collar of her blouse. I didn't feel much like laughing, either. I said, "It's okay! It's okay!" to her hair, her neck, and the collar of her blouse and walked back out of the foyer with the tables and the few chairs where the others were still drinking their coffee or beer, and didn't even wait until the beginning of the performance. I just wanted to get out of there and disappear. I looked up the way home on the city map and took the streetcar back to the apartment where the young director had cleared out a room for me.

There I sat down at his desk, paged through his books, and waited for him to come home and tell me that things hadn't been so bad after all.

When he did come back, I'd fallen asleep at his desk. He woke me and we went into the kitchen and ate stewed peaches because he couldn't find anything else in the refrigerator, and he told me that he, too, wished his debut as a director — up until then he'd just been an actor — had been a bit different, but that was one of the things you had to take in stride. The lead actress, however, had already been spoiled by success, which was why it was so hard for her. Hesitantly, he asked me if I knew that my father had made friends — in a manner of speaking — with that very same leading lady who'd done all the carrying on earlier in the evening. And then he gave me the letter that my father had left at the theater for me.

My Dear Daughter,

Forgive me for not coming to the station, but I'm feeling too poorly and I didn't want any 'last goodbyes.' As you're arriving in Frankfurt, I'll already be sitting in the train for Weimar. Probably we'll pass one another — maybe we could stick our tongues out at each other as we go by.

I've gotten the pains again, all over. When I get back, I'll probably have to go to the hospital, where they'll torture me even more. Slowly, I'm losing the courage to go through it again. What do I have to look forward to at eighty years? I'm upset, unhappy, if you want to call it that. All those questions of belief that I've wrestled with my entire life are now limited to the one simple certainty that is coming closer and closer.

Only once in my life was I as helpless and certain — during the war, in London, when two men in bowler hats

walked into my room and ordered me to pack up my things
and come along. (Believe me, at every time and in every
place, you're an enemy alien!) I was only allowed to call your
mother, with whom I'd been in love for just a few weeks, at
the factory where she was working. But they couldn't get
her to the phone and so all I could do was leave her a message that I had to go away for an indefinite period and
only God knew when and whether we'd see each other
again. Then, two years later, I came back from Canada.

　　What possessed me to travel to Frankfurt again for the
first time in fifty years, I really don't know. I wanted to see
everything again and relive old memories. But it's dangerous
to return to some remote place of childhood or youth, and,
almost as if I'd wanted to push the risk to the extreme, I
had arranged to meet Ruth here, because, back in those
days, we'd emigrated from this city together. You know I
hadn't seen her for decades and there I was, standing at
the airport, waiting for her. Then she came, almost a real
Englishwoman, and I thought for a moment what it would
have been like if I'd stayed there, too. An old woman with
white hair who was having a hard time dragging her suitcase from the carousel and getting it onto the baggage cart.
She was sweating and her clothes were wrinkled. Don't
think that's what bothered me — I know that I'm an old
man whose strength is leaving him, too. But under her arm
Ruth had a newspaper that I consider reactionary and I
said so right away, made some dumb remark about it, so
that Ruth got insulted and we started to argue while we
were still in the airport and criticized each other about our
different political opinions, just as we did fifty years ago
when we were still married and argued that way every
day. So I decided to drive Ruth to her hotel and tell her

45

that it was probably better if we each went our separate ways.
Why bother meeting when we still couldn't understand each
other? Life is already difficult enough for each of us and,
anyway, that kind of reunion with a friend from earlier
days, what good is it?

In the evening I went to the theater to see your play. I
was proud of you and wanted to meet the people who had
staged it. And then I even fell in love with the Correll wo-
man, the leading lady in your play. Maybe just because she's
from Frankfurt — from Wiesbaden, to be precise. During
the days that I had left here, I walked through both cities
with her and dragged her from one place full of memories
to another, which is what I had actually wanted to do with
Ruth. So I showed your leading lady my birthplace and
my father's sanatorium and the Sander family's banking
houses, which aren't in business anymore — they're called
"Deutsche Bank" and so on. The Correll woman shared
my overflowing emotions, because I did find a lot of things
again. It all soaked into my mood and
suddenly I had the feeling that ever since I'd left there, I'd
spent my whole life standing around in bad weather and
cold wind.

I hope while you're in Frankfurt you'll see the Palm
Garden, where your grandparents met at the Natural Sci-
entists' Ball, and the Senckenbergianum, where my grand-
mother once showed me, when I was a little boy, the reptiles
and the embryo collections, something she believed the son
of a natural scientist would probably be interested in.

Hopefully I'll get out of the hospital and be able to pull
myself together once more; then perhaps we'll see each other
again later — later in the year when you're already in
Paris, there or somewhere else. With all my heart I hope

*you'll hit it off better there. But anyhow, the way things
were, I always felt homeless.*

— *Your father*

I met up with the leading lady one more time at Café
Laumer, but she didn't feel like sitting there with me, didn't want
to talk about things, and drank her iced coffee in silence. But
then she suddenly asked me about Alfried, whether I knew him
from Berlin, and I said yes, of course I knew him from Berlin
and she told about the big hit she'd made in one of Alfried's
productions here — a wonderful piece of work. She wrote her
telephone number on a napkin for me, 5 89 21, said she had to
get going, and had already stood up and was running off. And
once again, I was seeing her only from the back, going down
the stairs of Café Laumer and suddenly all I could think of was
that she, too, had been Alfried's lover, at the same time when I
was writing him my letters that ended up in the dumpster.

I Iad my father said "Rheinstrasse" or "Steinstrasse" or "Wein-
strasse" when he was talking about the house where he was
born? I'd forgotten the name of the sanatorium, too. So I went
running around the villa district of Wiesbaden without knowing my way, just looking with astonishment at the place my
father came from, from such upper-middle class wealth, even if
it had long since trickled away. So much show and seriousness
that wasn't really quite genuine and perhaps had never been
genuine. But the city remained closed to me, simply an unfamiliar place; I walked along the twisting and turning streets
as I would have in any foreign city, gawked at the houses and
squares without any feeling for them, and hoped for a sign, any
sort at all, even if I had no idea where it might come from —
anything that could speak to me and tell me about my father as
a little boy and my great-grandparents and the bankers to the

grand dukes of Hesse-Darmstadt. But everything remained mute. So I just took in the rich, soft, indolent, somehow artificial atmosphere of the city, and the only thing I thought I could recognize again and again was a couple walking along in front of me, an old man and a young woman, walking along arm in arm or hand in hand, sometimes stopping to talk and sometimes kissing each other — my father and the leading lady in my play.

I even got on a tour bus. "The Bergstrasse, the Hessian mountain road — see it, experience it, make it your own." "Peaceful vineyard towns, strung together like pearls," said the tour guide. The excursion bus traveled down from Darmstadt to Heidelberg, first through Zwingenberg, where my grandmother Leonie was born, and then through the other towns along the Bergstrasse, where this or that ancestor had lived. I didn't know anything more exact about them, just that their ancestors had come up the Rhein valley with the Romans once upon a time — that's the way my father had told it, and he'd been proud of it.

In his historical ramblings, our tour guide mentioned the Romans and Celts, Allemanns and Franks, but didn't say a thing about my ancestors. On the other hand, he did point out the place where Siegfried was killed, and then the entire busload walked up from Heppenheim to Starkenburg, where lunch was served; and if you still felt like taking the trouble to climb up to the observation tower, you could see far out over the Rhein valley, or over to Odenwald on the other side. The tour guide was again recalling the deeds of the Nibelungs and I was thinking that somewhere over there had to be the Odenwald School, where my father was educated by the legendary Paul Geheeb, who was supposed to have said, "Nazis? Here in Hessia?"

Later, I looked around the little cemeteries for the graves of my grandparents and ancestors from the Bergstrasse, but couldn't find them, though there were names on many of the tombstones; or maybe that was the very reason, since I didn't know which of the many Weils and Sanders they were. I didn't know the dates they were born or died, hardly even a first name — didn't know anything about this family that had so many branches. I'd always looked upon my father as a single, solitary person who hadn't belonged to anyone. His family consisted only of his succession of wives; the court bankers whom he sometimes talked about were from another century. There just didn't seem to have been anyone more recent, more closely related, and I had no idea when or how that family tree had disintegrated and why my father never talked about it.

Finally I asked myself why I'd really gone there at all, to Frankfurt, to the Bergstrasse and Wiesbaden. Did I perhaps want to reassure myself, before I left for the longed-for foreign country, that I still had roots or a home town? But I didn't find out a thing, aside from my father's affair with the leading lady. My origins there had become completely invisible. I couldn't find a thing — not a memory, not a sign, not a memento, not a trace.

HERE THE POSTMAN simply stuffs my mail into the crack around the door, because there are no mailboxes for the basement apartments. The letters hang from the apartment doors like little flags. I see them even before I start down the steps. But my door is rarely decorated with little flags — my friends from Berlin have probably given up on me and my colleagues at the Berliner Theater are still talking in the canteen.

One day, however, a letter from Alfried was sticking in the door. I recognized his handwriting from a distance — how it reminded me of home! As I pulled the letter out, I saw that there was even a return address on it, a little white shield with his name, address, and telephone number. So now he was living in Munich. I wondered how he knew my address, but perhaps it's not only here that old friends ask each other, "Do you know him, do you know her?" Otherwise there really wouldn't be much to talk about, because the things that held us together earlier were now pulling us apart. As if it were turning out only now, in broad daylight, that we didn't really belong together at all, but earlier, when we constantly lived in an atmosphere of gloom, we simply hadn't noticed it.

Alfried had heard that I, too, had left the Berliner Theater and asked me in the letter why I'd gone to Paris, so far away, what I was doing there, and whether I wouldn't rather come to Munich where he could really help me find a job in the theater, and said that he'd like to see me again.

I was happy as I read the letter and no longer felt so alone. I left it lying on the table, the two pages open beside the envelope, so that the table was almost completely covered by Alfried's writing; he filled the whole room for a few hours. Later, in the evening, I read the letter again and felt very lonely and got home-sick. I sat down and wrote him an answer, a letter which — this time — I actually wanted to send.

> Dear Alfried,
>
> I've made a deep incision into my life and am still running around like I'm anesthetized and don't feel the pain. How shall I put it — I wanted to cut myself off, was sick of the old life and longed for some great change, a departure, a transformation. Perhaps the same thing happened to you back then. Now I'm already beginning to have my doubts, because I've found only a tiny apart-ment, which is halfway below ground level and even smaller than the one in Berlin. Instead of looking down at the streetcar terminal and the central stockyards, I now look up at the feet of people walking by.
>
> My street is one of those that lead to, or go out from, the Place d'Italie, depending on how you look at it; any-way, the square sits right in the middle and has spread out and holds a bundle of streets in its hand, several large

*avenues and a few ordinary streets, one of which leads to
the Chinese quarter. "Up there" it's pretty — at least it's
different and people speak a foreign language, French or
Chinese, so I feel like I'm left in peace.*

*I'd like to tell you about everything — yes, it would be
nice to see each other again. But I don't want to come to
Munich now that I'm here and I don't want to go back to
the theater, either — I'm through being an assistant. Now
that each of us is in an entirely different place, we could
— if we see each other again — compare what we've
found. We didn't just go into exile intending to go back
home again, we really emigrated, in order to start something completely new. Isn't that right?*

Instead of simply throwing it in the mailbox, I took the letter to the post office, because I suddenly wanted Alfried to get
it as quickly as possible, as if hours mattered now, in putting the
torn connection back together. For the first time in years, I was
thinking about Alfried again, as someone who was living somewhere, whom you could call up or visit. I imagined him taking
the letter out to the mailbox, then reading it, the sort of house
where that might be happening, on what sort of a street, and
what the city looked like.

Then, on my way to the French course at the community
college, I came across the poster, just a little poster, but it caught
my eye right away, even though there were only words on it. Before I'd really even read it, the unknown names on the other
posters were pushed aside by the familiar ones — Alfried's name,
the name of the author, the name of the play that Alfried had
staged years ago at the Berliner Theater.

I looked to see if perhaps the poster was still hanging there from the previous year, but no, it was for right now, for next week — a guest performance in Paris by the Munich Theater.

Alfried hadn't written a thing about it in his letter, hadn't mentioned the visit, as if he still wanted to keep himself hidden. So, without being invited, I went to the theater named on the poster and just took a seat in the darkened parquet during the dress rehearsal, in the last row, where Alfried couldn't see me. I heard the familiar language on stage, the well-known script that I still almost knew by heart, heard Alfried talking to the actors, sometimes yelling, and suddenly everything seemed as if we were still at the Berliner Theater. But I had indeed come through totally unfamiliar streets to that theater — which I didn't know at all — and on the Metro from Place d'Italie and not the number 57 bus from in front of my building. It wasn't the Berliner Theater and my brain was full of words in a foreign language that weren't falling out anymore, but getting all mixed up with everything else in my head, and I no longer knew where I was, or in what part of my life, and it made my head ache.

In the darkened theater I made a few sketches of Alfried, as I saw him there, indistinctly; just the way I still couldn't look the city right in the face, I preferred to draw Alfried from behind, in the dark, in quarter profile, before I actually saw him again.

When the rehearsal was over and the house lights came on, I called to him across the rows of seats and waved, but he acted as if he wasn't a bit surprised to see me there. We each ran out of our rows and met in the aisle beside the seats. We embraced, and I showed him the little drawing that I'd just made of him. He wanted me to give it to him, but I wouldn't.

I asked him why he hadn't mentioned anything in his letter about the guest performance and hadn't suggested meeting; but he just laughed and said that we'd always find each other and meet again, and that we couldn't lose each other. Making a date was completely unnecessary and the best proof of that was that there we were, standing together in the theater right then, and it was much more beautiful than any other way, right?

Then we left the theater and walked a bit through the city. I showed Alfried my apartment and my street and the Ecole des Beaux Arts where I was studying, and the community college where I was taking French. And I told him about my new life, and that he should see me in terms of that transformation, in terms of the freedom that I wanted to gain for myself here — here or somewhere else. But Alfried said there was no such thing as a new life, only the dream of a new life, the dream that you can start all over again from the very beginning, as another person with another name, in another form, in a completely different place, that you don't have to start over again at A, but can begin at B. But that was just an illusion. I told him that I knew he'd talk that way, but I was still a beginner at emigrating and couldn't learn all the lessons of my new life at once.

As we walked, we dragged our feet through the leaves that were lying there in a thick layer, and as we looked more closely we saw that they were ginkgo leaves; the long, straight avenue down which we were walking was lined by ginkgo trees. Alfried said that he didn't really like France and I felt like I was being attacked by such talk, as if he were reproaching me for living there now. So I started to say things against Germany, as Jean-Marc often did, and repeated some of those statements of his that I'd always rejected. We were attacking each other by finding fault with the countries in which we were living.

When we'd reached the end of the avenue, I asked Alfried if he still remembered the Ginkgo biloba at Belvedere that Goethe had planted, the one my father had showed us when we were visiting him one time, and how scruffy and unsightly the ginkgo looked there; and, here, they were just standing along the street by the dozens. Back then, in Belvedere Park, we'd each put a leaf of the Ginkgo biloba in our pockets. Did he still have his? No. And I didn't have mine, either; I'd thrown all of my dried plants out the window.

In a café we found a table directly in front of a window that reached right to the floor and sat down beside each other the way the French do, with a view of the street, the jostling crowd at the bus stop, and all the people who looked like they were really at home there, and then we went down the old list of names, asking each other what this one or that one was doing, colleagues or friends, whether they were still there or already gone and what had happened to them and from whom we'd heard the story. And once again, as he'd already done in his letter, Alfried asked me if I really didn't want to come to Munich and I said I didn't.

To get back to the theater we took the bus — line number 42 — that goes right by the laundromat where Jean-Marc was working. I could see him through the big window panes, talking with two Arabs inside. Probably they had stuffed the washing machines too full and now he was having to convince them that they'd be better off each using two machines with the load they had to do, if it wasn't something else they were discussing. Alfried was still talking about Munich; I didn't say anything to him about Jean-Marc.

At the theater, he quickly disappeared backstage where a whole bunch of people were already waiting for him, and I took a seat in the parquet that was now almost full. Nearly everyone sitting there was holding a piece of paper on which the familiar names were printed in big letters, as they were on the poster, Alfried's above all the rest. I was sad. Sad about our whole story, about our misunderstandings, and after the performance, even before the applause had died down and the lights came up again, I left the darkened theater and walked home, back to my thirteenth arrondissement, saw my street, the way it was lying there somehow unconscious, stretched out lengthwise and gray in the face. I walked down to my souterrain and pulled out of my pocket the little drawing I'd made of Alfried during the re-hearsal and put it up on the wall above my desk with a thumb-tack, next to the big map of Paris, and thought that things had probably always been that way between us — a love made out of nothing, in which nothing happens, and which endlessly fades away into nothingness.

DURING ONE OF THE rainy nights after fall had started —
my first fall in Paris — I dreamed that my father had gone
for a walk in Belvedere Park and hadn't come back. I was sitting
with his four wives, waiting for him, but he didn't come back,
never came back.

He'd just wanted to take an evening walk. There were so many
beautiful paths there, even some that were undiscovered and unknown, but many of them — especially if you followed Possen
Brook — led into the underbrush and swamps and then disap
peared. My father must have lost his way in there somewhere.
Days later, people came from Mellingen, the nearest village, and
said they'd found him in the swamp, beneath the underbrush that
reached down into the water and had concealed him. We'd better not look at him, the people from Mellingen told us, it was just
too awful, a person who'd been lying in the swamp so long, a
half-decayed person. But I was afraid they'd make me look at

him, that they'd say, "Go ahead and look, take a good look, and tell us who it is."

In the dream I believed that my father's wives had known everything and that my father had even wanted that kind of a death and had said so before he went out for his evening walk. But they'd excluded me from that ending. And in the dream I thought that if Bilbo, his dog, had still been alive, it wouldn't have happened, he would have fetched help and not simply watched while his master drowned or drowned himself and drifted into the underbrush in the swamp. But Bilbo had been dead for a long time by then.

On Sunday, at the laundromat, I told Jean-Marc about my dream. I said I'd dreamed that I'd become an orphan.

It was Jean-Marc's last Sunday at the laundromat — he'd only come back to pick up things of his that were still lying around there. He'd finished his studies and now he was going home. His parents urged him to every time they called and since they were already old and he was their only son, he gave in easily, now that he'd been away for years. I tried once more to get him to go with me to Weimar to visit my father, and to Berlin, so I could show him everything before he left Europe for good, but he refused, saying it was too late and besides, I knew he didn't want to.

He was already in the process of cleaning out his attic room, packing his suitcases, throwing things away, and I helped him wrap and tie the packages that we then took to the post office. The cleaned-out attic looked so forlorn. Jean-Marc had passed a few things on to me — the wicker chair and a table, in the drawer of which there were still the American magazines he was always reading, the Moulinex with which he sometimes sliced vegetables or mixed batter when he cooked supper for us, and some other little things that I could use. He helped me carry it all down to my souterrain.

Then he left. We'd no sooner gotten to know each other than there we were, saying goodbye again. I went with him to Charles de Gaulle Airport, where the flights leave for America, and told him we should have at least gone to the Atlantic coast together and stood by the open sea, on the last rock at the end of the continent, where you couldn't go any further. If I ever go to America, that's where I'd like to leave from on a ship, but there probably aren't any ships that sail to America anymore; they've probably long since gotten rid of them, like Ellis Island. There, at the end of the continent, where the landscape is said to be so wild, between the land and the water that's always rising and sinking and swaying, maybe we could have had some sort of adventure anyway, something else besides always just talking, speaking, telling — our eternal discussions. "Are you sorry you missed such an adventure, too, Jean-Marc?" I asked him, but he didn't answer, because the passengers for the Air France flight to New York were being told to proceed to gate 23 and no one else was allowed to go beyond security.

A few days later — actually at night — my father's wife called me. At least I have a telephone now, even if it doesn't ring very often because I still don't know that many people in Paris who'd want to call me and I really don't have the money for a long distance call to Berlin, and, anyway, what would we say?

"How are you? What're you doing?"

"How 'bout you?"

"What'd you do today?"

"How about this evening?"

"To the Berliner Theater?"

"What can I say?"

"Everything is different, more difficult, because being used to things makes everything seem easier."

"That's the way you wanted it."

"Sure I did. But try to understand."

"Your father is doing very poorly," my father's wife said on the phone. "They've sent him home from the hospital to die. He can't even move anymore and every now and then I have to turn him from one side to the other. He's in a lot of pain and cries when he thinks I'm not looking."

She was sleeping beside his bed on an air mattress so that she could comfort him at night or in case he needed something. Suddenly he'd start talking in a strange dialect — maybe from Frankfurt — which she didn't understand because she's from Brandenburg, so that sometimes she didn't even know what he wanted. She said he wouldn't live more than a few days.

"Later in the year," my father had said in the letter that's still in my handbag, "perhaps we'll see each other later in the year, after you've been in Paris for a while." Now things had already come to that point. It was almost winter. In the past few days I'd already seen boots on the legs walking past my window, the rain never seemed to stop, and it had even snowed a few times. But I wanted to see my father again, wanted to see him here. I'd meet him at the Gare de l'Est, I thought to myself, and lead him safely around the construction site to my apartment in the thirteenth arrondissement and borrow a folding bed from somewhere so he could spend the night at my place.

But all I could do was listen to his voice. His wife held the receiver to his ear when I called Weimar. I was hearing his voice again for the first time since I'd left, and for the last time as well. The first thing he did was to ask me about the leading lady, whether I'd seen her in Frankfurt and if I would call her, he could give me her phone number. "I know her number," I said. "She wrote it on a napkin for me at Café Laumer when we met there." I was insulted that all he talked about was his leading lady, and to hurt him I said, "When are you finally going to visit

me, when are you coming here?" so that he had to tell me himself that he was dying. So weak that he couldn't move and
couldn't even hold a ballpoint pen to write a letter — just
imagine being so weak. Said he'd hoped he'd still have a little
time left, at least one or two years, perhaps one or two years
wasn't really asking too much. But now he knew he didn't have
any more time left. "Now we have to hang up," said my father
on the phone. But how were we supposed to hang up? I
couldn't cry or scream over the phone, and even if he'd been
standing in front of me, would I have been able to hug him and
kiss him? "Well, okay," is what we said on the phone and that's
the way it was, our farewell. "We've got to hang up now, so long
then," is what we said and then we hung up at each end.

During the following days I stayed in my apartment and
didn't go out of the building at all, just sat there and waited and
looked at the feet that were walking by my window, and asked
myself where they were all running off to and why no one who
belonged to those feet came in to see me. I frittered the day
away, hardly moving, and it was so quiet in the building that I
could hear the telephones ringing in the neighboring apartments and even on other floors. I twisted and turned around
and listened to them, frightened, because I expected the news
of my father's death from every telephone. When my own
phone — which was sitting on the floor so that I had to kneel
down to pick up the receiver — finally did ring, I thought to
myself, "Why bother, the ringing itself is telling me that my
father's dead." But of course I had to talk to his wife and find
out when he was going to be buried and ask her if she'd wait
until I could get a visa or permission to reenter the country to
at least attend the funeral.

And there was no one I could talk to about it; no one in my
entire thirteenth arrondissement knew anything about my

father, and yet he'd really lived in this city, had walked around here fifty years ago with his first wife, my mother's predecessor, and had sat in libraries and written articles for the *Vossische Zeitung* and visited people or met them in a café — people who also hadn't been around for a long time and whom no one remembered.

I dug all of my father's letters out of the cardboard boxes, unfolded them, and laid them on top of each other, so I could page through them and read them as if they were a novel. There were even letters from my childhood, from the time with my mother, letters that he'd written to me in summer camp, and some from the time with the actress, with her greetings added underneath. Once they'd been in Yugoslavia and once in Austria. And letters from the time with his last wife in Belvedere Palace and the one with the Hölderlin verse where he'd underlined "murder" — which was the last page of the novel.

I saw his writing on the paper and heard his voice in my ear — even though his wife had told me that my father's body was dead now, which meant his voice as well. But I still heard it; it was in my head there in my basement apartment, and it left the building with me and rode around the thirteenth arrondissement and all over the whole city with me — so you really couldn't say that everything had been extinguished. I could hear the way he'd said "If I just had one or two more years, perhaps one or two more years wouldn't be asking too much," the way he was willing to settle, in desperation, for such a tiny amount, as if he'd be granted a postponement or receive an extension if he were satisfied with something absolutely minimal. That's the way I'd beg Alfried when he'd come at night and just stay for such a short time: "Stay at least five more minutes!" He'd laugh at me. "Why do you say five minutes when you really mean that I should stay for a long time, possibly forever? You want to

extort your excessive demand with an apparently modest request, but you know I'm not going to stay for long and certainly not forever, that I'm just stopping by for a little while, and
then I'm going to leave again, and sometime it'll be all over —
you know that, that's the way it is, you can't change it. This
longing to be together is like longing for eternal life — a childish dream."

When I lay in bed at night, I couldn't help lying on my back
as rigidly and motionlessly as my father must have done when
he wasn't able to turn over any longer and I stayed that way and
didn't move until it hurt. I forced myself to stay in that position
without changing, absolutely motionless, as if I had to wait for
someone to come and turn me, until I finally moaned out loud
from the pain and stiffness, and thought I'd been able to sense a
little of his suffering by torturing myself, and I finally cried, too,
and at least was relieved by crying. Because for my whole life
I'd been afraid I wouldn't have any tears and wouldn't be able
to cry on the day my father died. When I finally did fall asleep,
my father would appear in my dreams — there he was, alive
again, talking to me and telling me something very important,
something he only ever told me in dreams. We'd be sitting in
Belvedere Palace or in my apartment in Berlin or standing in
the wings of the Berliner Theater, between the audience and
the big door through which they carried the sets in and out,
and sometimes we'd be walking in the orangery or past the
Ginkgo biloba, calling Bilbo, our dog, who, once again, didn't
want to keep up with us. The dog's name would change into
my own and I'd hear my father calling my name until I woke
up. Then my father would be dead again and it was totally
impossible for me to imagine that now he was in the cold earth
or another world.

THERE WAS STILL a gigantic construction site at the Gare de l'Est, but of course now I knew which door to use to get in. From the Gare de l'Est I traveled back to the east again, from Gare de l'Est to Frankfurt and from Frankfurt to Weimar. I stood on the platform at the Frankfurt Hauptbahnhof again, as I had a few months earlier, when I'd looked for my father and called out to him in vain. There were still five hours until the train left for Weimar, in the middle of the night. In my pocket I had a telegram: "Request for visa granted" — just a note, a scrap, like the one with which they let me out.

I stepped into a telephone booth and called Wiesbaden 5 89 21 to tell the leading lady that my father had asked about her shortly before his death, but she wasn't at home, only one of the other apartment residents, who asked whether he could take a message. Yes, I said, my father, whom perhaps he'd seen when he was visiting in Wiesbaden, was dead. The man from the apartment said, "Oh, I'm sorry to hear that," and I asked him to leave a note for the actress. I threw the napkin with her telephone number into the wastepaper basket.

I took a look at the shops in the station and drank a cup of tea and, an hour later, a cup of coffee, and then another cup of tea. Later, I bought a sandwich at a stand and sat down on a bench, then on a different one, because I was afraid of falling asleep. The whole railroad station seemed changed since I'd arrived back then, maybe only because it was daytime then and nighttime now, and now I could see people who were lying in corners or prowling around — poor people, homeless people, or drunks I hadn't noticed at all previously and who scared me now. Because it was getting close to Christmas, the whole station was fancied up with evergreen boughs and Christmas ornaments, little bells and imitation snow, which didn't fit with all the dirt and the nighttime suspicion — it looked ridiculous and everything gave the impression of exhaustion and being close to the end.

As if I'd been tagged out in a game, I was making the whole trip again in reverse, the way it says in the rules — the player returns to the starting place and play begins again — with all the same stations: Place d'Italie — Gare de l'Est — Metz — Frankfurt — Eisenach — Erfurt — Weimar. The way I'd come. It seemed as if they didn't want to let go of me there, as if I were supposed to look at everything again — but perhaps in a more conciliatory mood — and ask myself why I'd gone away in the first place.

The broad avenue that leads up to Belvedere Palace culminates in a magnificent approach onto a square with a fountain that leaps up from a basin bordered by wild roses. On both sides of the palace are the courtiers' cottages in which a music school is housed, so that all over the park and palace grounds, from somewhere or other depending on how the wind's blowing, you can always hear snatches of music — a violin, a few plinks on the piano, sometimes even singing.

For years it had been said that a museum was going to be established in the palace, and for years my father's wife had been preparing for the installation of that museum. But only rarely did any carpenters come. They'd get started on something in several rooms, then stop right in the middle of whatever they were working on, leaving things lying all over the place, and go off, never to be seen again. For several weeks the roofers were busy putting on copper sheathing, but they hadn't even finished half of one wing when they disappeared, simply leaving the other half of the roof uncovered. And they never came back, either. So the palace had always remained empty, half dilapidated and half restored. Nothing was ever installed in it and my father and his wife were completely alone during all the years they lived there.

Before the funeral, my father's coffin was on view in one of the empty rooms with big mirrors and fireplaces, in between the coveralls and shoes that the workers had left lying around, and the janitor of the music school — who'd always called my father "Izzy" behind his back — apparently came over and said, "So long, Chief."

My father led a totally retiring life in Weimar. He no longer went to the party meetings, not even to the meetings of Victims of the Nazi Regime, but nevertheless they continued to send printed birthday greetings to their "Dear Comrade" or "Dear Colleague," respectively, even after his death. He didn't participate in the social life of his young wife, who, as a museum director, was always being invited somewhere. For the most part, he didn't even pick up the telephone and if the bell rang down at the palace gate, he'd stick his head out of the window — because the intercom hadn't worked for years — and yell down, "No, no, there's no one here." He didn't want to see anyone anymore. Instead of his own memoirs, he wrote a few biographies of people who were as unlike him as you could imagine and who didn't interest him in the least, and they were published by a firm that he looked down on because of their other publications.

More than anything else, he went walking in the park and played a childish game with his dog, who was called Biloba, after the ginkgo. He'd climb up into a gigantic, old tree that was hollowed out and whose thick branches spread almost to the ground, so that it was like a fortress with outer courtyards; then my father would barricade himself in there and let the dog look for him.

When I visited him, he'd show me around the orangery first, where rare and exotic trees were growing — in summer they'd even be brought outside — cedars of Lebanon, orange and carob trees and palms, and my father would complain over and over again about the scruffy condition of the Ginkgo biloba and the other trees from foreign countries that never bore fruit. Then we'd walk on, to the grottos and fountains and the artificial ruins and over to Possen Brook, which ran along the park, and then across the bridge and into the woods. Sometimes if night came on quickly — even though we'd only wanted to take an evening stroll — we'd get lost in the woods on the far side of the park and would stumble over branches and roots, unable to find our way, because we were really city people and weren't used to seeing at night and finding our way out there in the wilds. Most of the time the dog deserted us as well and raced back and forth through the woods and all we could hear was his distant, frantic barking. Having rediscovered his hunting dog's instincts, he'd go flushing out nocturnal animals and didn't want to follow us anymore, wouldn't even let us catch a glimpse of him, and we'd be afraid — for him and of the animals of the night and also that we wouldn't be able to find our way back to the palace without him. We'd yell and scream "Bilbo!" — because his name had long since been shortened — "Bilbo, come here! Come, Bilbo!"

"Actually, your father died of starvation and thirst," is what his wife told me after the funeral. He couldn't eat or drink any longer, or didn't want to, and she'd tried to feed him cream of wheat and tea with a teaspoon and counted off the spoonfuls the way you would to a little child. "One more spoonful, come on, a spoonful for you, a spoonful for me, and a spoonful for your daughter, a spoonful for Bilbo, a spoonful for your Mama and one for your Papa, and a spoonful for the court bankers, a spoonful for the Bergstrasse, a spoonful for the Odenwald School, please, a spoonful for the *Vossische Zeitung*, a spoonful for Paris, a spoonful for London, a spoonful for Berlin, a spoonful for the new Germany, a spoonful for the Victims of the Nazi Regime, a spoonful for Belvedere Palace and a spoonful for the Ginkgo biloba, please, please!"

"That was all just like it was with *Martha*," I told her and she asked who Martha was and what was this business about Martha. Perhaps my father had never told her the story about *Martha*.

We were standing in his room, which I'd wanted to see once more. I poked around in his things, saved his Russian watch for myself, and took his English notebook with the pocket calendar from the year 1944 from the drawer of his desk. My father had transposed the weekdays to the year 1946, the year in which he'd returned to Germany. The name of each weekday had been crossed out and the right one entered beside it, but only a few pages had been written on, and on those few pages there were mostly just a few lines in the middle. I read them through, right there in my father's room under the roof of Belvedere, next to Goethe's and Karl August's dumbwaiter, "table-set-yourself."

★ ★ ★

[WEDNESDAY] May 31. *Friday*

With Military Entry Permit No. 17174 and Certificate of Identity No. H5139, I crossed the German border on May 23, coming from London via Prague.

All in all, I've been away for thirteen years, and now I'm coming back to Berlin and the Russians, although the English are expecting me in Hamburg.

[THURSDAY] June 1. *Saturday*

Pick up my luggage from Zoo Station with the party's car. The chauffeur is a nice fellow. We drive through Lützowstrasse; he tells me about the last of the fighting around the bunker near the zoo. At party headquarters, I have to wait for hours to talk to F. Questions me in detail about my party career, has my file brought in, and writes down what's new. Provides a letter in which I make a declaration to the English that I'll be staying in the Russian zone. Asks me what I want to do there, laughs when I say, "Start a newspaper."

[SATURDAY] June 3. *Monday*

Sign up for rooms and ration cards. Leave the dormitory with my two roommates who are from Chemnitz, go to a bar they know. Nothing but drunken women. Awful. (Saw W. U.'s twelve-cylinder Mercedes.)

[SUNDAY] June 4. *Tuesday*

Moved to Building V, room 3. Nothing accomplished at the housing office in Pankow. Stand in line. District Supervisor Krause takes his time. Get my ration cards and buy something for the first time — a little butter, cookies, sugar, and concentrated soup. Supper at the K.'s, listen to some awful, sentimental records afterward. Drive to Ostkreutz, from there an hour on the trolley, then from Alexanderplatz on foot, accompanied against my will by a man who tells about the attack on Feb. 3 and is worried about Germany because there's not enough room.

[MONDAY] June 5. *Wednesday*

Get something to eat on my ration card. Lots of pointless walking around. Housing office, again no luck. Evening in the Fürstenhof, again mainly drunken women and men, see party officials right smack in front of me. A lot of schnapps. Hungry and sad. But pretty good oompah music.

[THURSDAY] June 8. *Saturday*

Long line in front of the butcher shop, leave again. Housing office — no luck. Return to the butcher's and get my first sausages. Then go for a bath, a line again, foreigners allowed in first. Some grumble, so they get told about what they've done to other countries, now they just have to wait. People without a country, like I am, are considered foreigners and are permitted to bathe ahead of the Germans.

Regine visits me in the dormitory of building IV and brings an electric kettle and a cup and makes me some tea. Later we take a walk on Hasen Heath and at night I wander from Küstriner Platz to the Brandenburg Museum. Moon above the street, no other light, and long, long stretches of nothing but ruins. Scary.

Go by bicycle along the east-west connector to Kurfürstendamm. At the Russian Memorial, Red Army men are dropped off by trucks — they're taking group pictures. Americans take snapshots from their jeep without getting out. Take a look at the bunker near the zoo and the little cemetery for the people killed on the eighth of May. Drink a lemonade at Café Vienna.

[FRIDAY] June 9. *Sunday*

In the communal kitchen of Building IV. Yefim comes. We talk about our lost illusions. Evening together in the Fürstenhof. The Germans in high spirits again. Yefim in civilian clothes. Someone asks us if we're Italian. They no longer remember what Jews look like.

[SATURDAY] June 10. *Monday*

Try to write my first articles. Turns out to be hard for me. To Police Headquarters for my papers. Across from me, among the detectives, a young boy who ran away from Beuthen to look for his father who's supposed to be in a camp — doesn't know where or why. But perhaps Berlin tempted him, too. They say the Amis give the children as much chocolate as they want. He's really disappointed. Spent four nights bumming around somewhere and fell asleep in Alex in broad daylight from hunger and exhaustion. Now he's going to be put in a home.

Evening at Circus Barley. Lions, elephants, and tricks on the unicycle, but everything much too serious. The guy on the unicycle ought to at least smoke a cigarette at the same time. Walk home, sad, not quite sure where I am. A little bit like the Italian in the circus, who's really from Russia. Just as much of an Italian as I am.

★   ★   ★

That was all my father had entered in his pocket calendar. Aside from that, there was just a section for addresses full of names that didn't mean a thing to me and a table for converting English weights and measures into the European metric system.

Because I didn't want to take the calendar back to Paris with
me just as a memento, and because there were so many empty
pages, I wrote my own continuation in it and transposed the
weekdays to the current year once more. I entered the day my
father died and the day of his funeral and the day when we'd
seen each other for the last time and then I started to fill up the
empty pages, so that our notes ran into each other in the English pocket calendar that was long out of date as it was.

★   ★   ★

[FRIDAY] December 15. *Tuesday*
Weimar, Apolda, Naumburg, Weissenfels, Halle, Berlin. I've
traveled this stretch hundreds of times, but now the trip is ille-
gal, because the "permit" is only valid for the place of the
funeral.

For that reason I got out of the train somewhere on the edge
of Berlin, in order to go on by subway or bus, because I thought
I'd be less likely to call attention to myself that way. Got lost right
away because I'd never been in that part of town before. It was a
totally unfamiliar district — the first time I'd laid eyes on it. A
street sign pointed to the Autobahn in the direction of Fürsten-
walde, a name I knew well. We may have driven by there a long
time ago, when I was a child and still living with my parents.
They had a house on Scharmützelsee where we spent our weekends. I can't really remember, only what my parents told me
about it — a little wooden villa with a veranda that looked out
on the lake, a big garden with old trees, a few beds with beans,
and strawberries, raspberry bushes and apple trees, and a swing
in front of the kitchen window. They claimed that Johannes R.
Becher did calisthenics with me whenever he came over in his
sailboat and then they'd sit under the trees in lawn chairs and

discuss how things ought to be done in the new Germany. About that time I wanted to become a botanist and I hunted for specimens in the garden or at the water's edge; when I wanted to extend my investigations using Johannes R. Becher's sailboat, of course that was forbidden. The house and garden had been leased and after just a few years, the owner — whom my father always referred to as "that old Nazi" — demanded to have them both back. From then on there was no more house and garden on Scharmützelsee, my parents soon separated, the actress didn't need a weekend house, because, as it was, she always had something to do at the theater, and my mother was probably already thinking about going back to Bulgaria.

Many years later, while I was at the university, I actually did go back to that town. My girlfriend's mother had a house there, almost a manor, and my girlfriend and I spent a lot of weekends there, sometimes with her mother or with friends, or with her mother's friends. It was a sort of refuge from life in Berlin and life in general. We let ourselves be pampered by her mother and her friends, but we weren't comfortable with the pampering, either, because it really did seem like a way of getting us to keep quiet, silencing us. Then we'd run away again. One time I showed my girlfriend the house and garden at the other end of town that had been our house and garden once upon a time, and behind the fence we saw the "old Nazi" working in his garden. We went running off to the Rauen Hills — whose name was practically the only one from around there that had stayed in my memory since childhood — or took one of the three paths that led to the neighboring villages; soon we knew every stone that lay there and every bush that grew there, and began to dream of things far away and unknown, and we wanted to go roaming far and wide and cooked up great plans for our lives.

[SATURDAY] December 16. *Wednesday*

Every old man I see on the street frightens me. I look at him and think, "Why is he alive but doesn't know me and why is he walking by without looking at me, as if I don't mean a thing to him, why can't he be my father?" Then I start to blubber from grief over the fact that every journey is senseless, now that I'll never be able to find my father again. No matter where I go, I still won't find him again — anywhere, ever, not when times are good or when they're bad.

On every corner there's an apartment where someone I know lived or still lives. "Should I go in?" I ask myself each time, but walk by quickly.

[SUNDAY] December 17. *Thursday*

Next to the S-Bahn station on Lenin Avenue, Werner Seelenbinder Hall stretches out disconsolately, once again — or still — getting ready for some Party celebration or other, the central stockyard stinks, and the streetcars go squealing into the terminal and out again. I went to my old apartment. Actually, to be honest, I sneaked in to see what sort of name was on my door now. There it was: "Walter." Mr. or Mrs. Walter has finally had a doorbell installed, something I hadn't managed to accomplish in ten years — people always had to knock. Then I stood at the bus stop in front of my door and waited for the number 57 and rode to the Berliner Theater to take a look at the posters and see what play they were rehearsing, who had what roles, and who the dramaturges, alternates, and assistants were. I stood in front of the list of all those familiar names for quite a while, until the doorman asked me if I wanted to speak with someone, saying they were all in rehearsal right then, until two o'clock. After that I could find them all in the canteen. I knew that, of course. I didn't want to talk to anyone. I said "Thanks."

Found a seat in the Lindenkorso and wrote postcards like a tourist — one with a photograph of the Berliner Theater to Alfried in Munich — and a letter to Jean-Marc in New York.

> *Dear Jean-Marc,*
> *God only knows when I'll know what has happened. I'm in Berlin now, where you never wanted to go. My father died. He was buried in Weimar, not far from Belvedere Palace.*
> *A young woman with a child has moved into your apartment under the eaves and she doesn't know what to make of it when I try to help her out. At the laundromat, a Chinese, or someone who looks like one, has your old job. Now I'm sorry that we always spoke to each other in a foreign language and only the words that we had to invent to be able to do that still seem to have any meaning for me.*
> *I'm slowly making progress in painting from nature and even have enough confidence in myself to go out and paint — if not actually the city, at least a few trees or the grass. I have to get out of the basement. Maybe I should have moved into your attic — up there is certainly better than half underground. Hugs from Berlin!*

[MONDAY] December 18 *Friday*

I didn't go to see a single person in Berlin, not one of my old friends and not even my coworkers at the Berliner Theater. In the hours just before my train left, I went to places where no one lives anymore — to the building where my mother lived before she moved back to Bulgaria and the one where I visited my father at the actress's apartment. She's still living there. As had been the case in Paris, however, every presence had been wiped away and even the memories, it seemed to me, couldn't

75

really be associated with those places. Suddenly, as I was standing there in front of those buildings, the leaving and returning and the friendships and the different places in the world seemed robbed of any sense, as if they all dissolved or flew off into the air whenever you tried to approach them and you never actually knew whether they'd just evaporated or whether you, yourself, were running away.

I took along a few of the Ginkgo biloba's leaves from Belvedere Park again and stuck them into my coat pocket. In time, the leaves will crumble and disintegrate as I reach into my pocket over and over, and they'll get mixed together with the crumbs down there and I won't take the coat to the cleaner's so that the leaf dust will stay at the bottom of the pocket.

At Friedrichstrasse station, right in front of the border crossing, I met Wanda, someone I knew from the theater. We stopped and talked to each other on the street and I could tell that she didn't even know I wasn't living there anymore — and I didn't tell her.

I couldn't make myself look at the entire stretch from Berlin to Frankfurt to Paris again. Took the sleeping car and lay down and closed the curtains.

Theatre   refusal of repetition

+ refusal to observe

↳ freedom of starting

vs - repeating parents' past

ZOHARA'S JOURNEY

ACKNOWLEDGMENT

*The translator wishes to thank Rabbi Alan Fuchs
for his generous and invaluable advice.*

I CRIED FOR THREE DAYS and three nights and didn't say a thing to anyone, but kept everything to myself. I sat in our bedroom the whole day staring at the children's empty beds and asking myself what had happened. But then I told Frau Kahn everything. I met her in front of the elevator about nine o'clock, just as I was about to take out my trash. She's been my neighbor for a long time and has been through a lot herself in those terrible camps, so she'd be able to handle it, I thought. She tried to comfort me and came over to my place. We sat down in the kitchen and she got me to take twenty of her drops and said that things would soon be all right again. "We'll get them back again for sure, Frau Serfaty — for sure!"

Simon had said we were going to take a trip, go on vacation. But we never went on vacation, at least not together. Only the two bigger girls got to go to summer camp last year, although they both protested at first, Zippora because she was too big for such things, Elisheva because she was too little. The congregation had offered two places free of charge at the summer camp run by the B'nai Akivah — they're religious, you can trust them — and I thought it would be good for the girls to get away for a while, get a chance to breathe the good, clean air in the Alps, and a little peace and quiet wouldn't hurt me, either. But when they were actually gone, time seemed to pass very slowly without the two girls and every day I went running out to meet the mailman, to ask if there was anything for me. Right here, above the kitchen table where we eat, one of their postcards is still hanging; on it there are huge mountains of gray rock, flat moss, and grass. You can see a little river as well, and there's snow up above on the mountains. I don't think mountains are beautiful — they scare me. The sea is my landscape. In Oran, the sea was all there was. I don't know the mountains.

When the girls finally came back from summer camp, I stood on the platform with the other parents, waiting for them, and as the train came into the station, all the mothers and fathers started to run with the train, alongside the cars from which the children were waving, and then the train finally stopped and the screaming and yelling started: "Yoo-hoo, David! Yoo-hoo, Chaya! Here we are! Here Ilan! Yoram, over here!" They were all pushing and shoving and running toward each other and they were almost all crying as they threw their arms around their children.

I was absolutely astonished when Simon said he wanted to take a trip with us. For the past two years he'd hardly even been here, but, instead, was always traveling around the world collecting money for the Jews in Russia, for the Jews in Syria, and for the Yeshivas in Israel, for cemeteries, schools, and Torah scrolls. He collected for every conceivable religious purpose, was constantly on the move, on every continent, from one end to the other. He collected money for everyone — we were the only ones to whom he didn't send a thing. Nothing for me and nothing for the children. We live on the allowance for children and the housing allotment, and health insurance for me and the children is covered by the French government as well, thank God. One of the children is always sick — sore throats, earaches, they're always falling down — at least once a week I have to call Dr. Schwab to come and see someone. He knows I have worries about money and always writes out the receipt for the health insurance ahead of time, so I don't have to pay him until I've gotten the refund money.

In the last few years, Simon would sometimes call and say he was passing through, would be there for one or two hours — he'd just arrived on the train, in Kehl, I should bring the children to the station quickly so we could see each other, as if he couldn't risk crossing the border himself and had something to fear on this side.

Once or twice a neighbor drove me over, but if I couldn't find anyone, I had to take a taxi, just leave everything right where it was and herd the children together as if there were a fire alarm.

Then Simon would be standing in the waiting room beside the newspaper kiosk, and we'd take our places around him and he'd hold court like the Sun King and ask us all sorts of questions and lecture us about worldly things and especially, of course, about religious ones, after which he'd go rushing off again, without a word of explanation about where he'd come from, where he was going, or about his perpetual absence and why he no longer came across the border to visit us at home. We were never allowed to accompany him out onto the platform. We just turned right around again and marched back across the Rhine Bridge, where it's always so windy that at least one of the children and sometimes I, myself, would arrive on the opposite side thoroughly chilled. Behind the little customs house, we'd walk down the steps and take the number 2 bus back home.

And now he'd told me we were going on a vacation trip. I was to pack things for the children and myself and come over to Kehl again, to the Europa Hotel, not to the railroad station — we'd spend the night there and be on our way the following day, on the train. I asked him where we were going and why we couldn't just spend the night in our apartment, but he got nasty right away and told me not to ask such stupid questions and just do what he told me. So I got everything together, a pile of underwear, socks, sweaters, pants, and shoes, and each of the children added something more that just had to be taken along — toys and books and whatnot. They were so thrilled to be going on vacation. Then we took the bus across the Rhein to Kehl; he was actually waiting for us at the Europa Hotel, and we spent the night at the hotel, in rooms across the hall from one another, he in one room with the boys and I in the other with the girls.

The following morning, however, I noticed that in all the confusion of getting ready, I'd left the first aid kit at home — a bag full of suppositories, drops, pills, cough medicine, and band-aids, anything that might be needed. Dr. Schwab got it all together for us "just in case." I said to Simon, "I have to get that bag, because we can't go anywhere without it — I'll take the bus right away and be back again in half an hour and then we can be on our way." I hurried as fast as I could, took the 10:02 bus from the bridge, managed to catch the 10:26 from our corner, and at eleven on the dot I was back in the hotel again. By then it had happened. They weren't in the lobby, not in the rooms, not in the breakfast room, either — they weren't anywhere. It was as if they'd never been there at all. I asked the woman at the registration desk. "No," she said, "the man left nothing behind. Yes, he asked me to tell you that you can go home." And that's what he — who can't speak German — was supposed to have said to this woman who doesn't understand French? How? What's that supposed to mean? What kind of craziness is this? I screamed and cursed, probably in Arabic. Arabic curses are about all that's left from our time living among the Arabs. The woman got upset and started to make telephone calls — maybe she wanted to get the police, maybe I'd screamed too loudly, maybe she was afraid I was going crazy, right there in front of her in the Europa Hotel. An Arab woman going crazy, that's all she needed. So I bit my tongue and clawed the arm of the easy chair. Then my things fell, the pouch with the pills and drops plopped out, the cough medicine bottle skittered across the floor and broke and the syrup ran onto the carpet in a sluggish stream. I had to crawl around on my knees to scrape it all together, pick up the glass slivers and wipe up the syrup — my hands got sticky, everything stuck together, and then I really felt like cursing. Cursing and howling.

The woman behind the registration desk stopped paying attention to me. So much the better! I went on sitting in the chair in the hotel lobby until evening. Now and then I ran over to the station to at least give myself something to do. As if they might suddenly come back after all, on some train or other, from somewhere. Trains did arrive, from places I don't know, and left in one direction or another for places I don't know either. People got in, said goodbye, yelled things to each other through the windows — the kinds of things people say when they part, trivial things: *say hello to, be careful of, remember* Other people got out of the trains and hurried over to the buses or taxis; some were being met — women by their husbands or children by their parents — but they all went off quickly in their own directions and I stood there, inundated, then cast aside again by the meetings taking place around me. Then I went back to the hotel and sat down again in the easy chair opposite the door. I thought maybe he'd call. People came and went, and some even sat down for a while in one of the chairs beside me and smoked and waited and then left again and no one asked me a thing and no one said anything to me and no one saw what was going on within me. After eight hours of waiting — it was exactly seven in the evening — Simon actually did call. The woman at the registration desk showed me to the phone and I started screaming right away — what was going on, where was he, what was he thinking of and what was going to happen now, why did he just leave with the children at exactly the right moment, had he arranged it that way ahead of time, there was absolutely no point to it, what good was it going to do him, it was just plain crazy, more of his damned theatrics. He growled like a dog, then barked — I should stop speaking to him in that tone, what would the people in the hotel think when they heard me screaming on and on like that, didn't I have any respect for him. "I am traveling on with the children now. Go home!" is what he said, then hung up.

Then I probably fainted. The woman at the registration desk managed to put on a sympathetic expression afterward, as if she wanted to ask, "What are you going to do now?" I told her not to worry, I was really leaving, I was going home.

But go home where? Without my children I no longer had a home.

WE HAVE A three-room apartment. In the bedroom where I slept with Simon is our big double bed and a dressing table with a large mirror, which I've never used because I just don't have time to spend looking at myself in the mirror and arranging my hair, and, besides, I've always worn a kerchief on my head. It's a long time since I've used that room, because Simon hasn't come home for such a long time that you can hardly call it a marriage any longer. Am I supposed to get into that big bed all alone?

I moved in with the children. All seven of us slept in their room. The room had wallpaper with little butterflies that I'd concentrate on whenever I couldn't go to sleep, which happened fairly often, unfortunately. Some of the butterflies had spots on their wings and some had none, and I used to try to figure out whether there were more with spots or more without spots.

In the former bedroom we threw all of our clothing onto the former marriage bed, where it grew into big heaps and mounds, which the mirror over the dressing table transformed into a whole mountain range; besides that, we stored anything else there we didn't need at the moment, anything superfluous that was standing around and getting in the way. In time, the bedroom was transformed into a junk room, a hall of mirrors of my bad memories.

The children do their homework in the living room, at the big table where we eat on the Shabbat. A couple of armchairs are arranged along the wall, where I sit and sew or darn or fold the wash and supervise the children's homework, trying to keep them from quarreling or at least to settle their arguments so they can go on working in peace and quiet. Ruth, the youngest of the girls, and Jonathan, the smallest of the boys — the smallest one of all — are always fighting about something and can't leave each other alone. Sometimes I have to send one of them into the kitchen. On the Shabbat I stretch out in one of the easy chairs after we've eaten and take my siesta. No one is allowed to disturb me. During the week we eat in the kitchen.

Since I've had the children, I'm never alone anymore. Not an hour, not a minute, not a moment. I've always had the children around me. In all the tiny apartments in all the cities where we've lived — in Amiens, in Marseille, in Nice, in Orleans, in Angers, in Nantes, in Lille, in Metz, and finally in Strasbourg. Like all Algerians, I would like to have stayed in Marseille or Nice, of course, because those cities remind me most of Oran and because they have streets where it smells the way my whole childhood smelled — of mint and cumin.

Why did Simon always have to move from one city to another? It was as if he were always looking for something or, on the other hand, as if he were running away from something. He never explained. That's just the way it was, it had to be that way, and I followed him. I never got to know any of those cities well at all and never really met a single person there. Always just made my rounds, from home to kindergarten, to school, to the store, to the doctor, the synagogue, take the children somewhere, pick them up, take them back again, pick them up again, parents' meetings, trips, plays, always dragging the smallest ones with me, at least as long as I couldn't leave them alone. Dress them, button them up, tie their shoes, undo their buttons, take off their clothes, untie their shoes, put everything back again. Everything always revolved around the children and the children were always where I could see them. I tried to protect them from everything bad, from all the unimaginably horrible things that could happen to someone, things you sometimes experience in nightmares. You wake up and scream. Jonathan had several of those bad dreams in the weeks just before vacation and screamed "Mama! Mama!" in the middle of the night and I ran over to his bed, stroked his head and covered him up again and whispered to him, "I'm here, I'm here." And each time, Ruth, who sleeps next to him, would grumble in a loud whisper, "Stop carrying on!" Maybe Jonathan sensed that something bad was coming. In any case, I had no inkling, or at least no idea that it would be like going over a cliff, because I thought that my measure of unhappiness was already full, with a husband who was never there, a father who didn't care about his children, an invisible rabbi. During all those years I lived only for my children, and my life was actually transformed into the life of my children, and without the children I was nothing any longer, simply nothing.

"HE MUST HAVE mentioned the name of some town or other," Frau Kahn said over and over again, "he has to have said something about where he was going with the children. A city, a country, a region, at least he must have indicated the direction. I mean, you say you're going south, to the Mediterranean, to the mountains, or to some town or other."

"No, nothing," I said, "I really can't remember anything."

Frau Kahn tried to squeeze it out of me, but it didn't work, I just didn't know anything more. All I could come up with was something like "Kehl."

"Maybe he said Kehl." But Frau Kahn thought that was totally ridiculous — we were in Kehl already. "Perhaps he said Cologne?"

"Kehl, Cologne — he's dragged my children off, they're gone, I don't know where."

Frau Kahn told me to calm myself, we'd think about it some more, we'd do everything possible, but first we'd have to go over

things to figure out a way. She got an atlas and showed me
where Cologne was, up there in Germany, you had to go up the
Rhine. I asked her if it was kosher there, he'd only take the children to some place that was kosher. All she said was, "Oh God,
no!" but then I saw on the map that Antwerp wasn't very far
away, the most orthodox place in all of Europe. "But that's no
place to take children on vacation," said Frau Kahn. I asked Frau
Kahn to do something, telephone, call up Germany; after all, the
last news had come from Germany, from Kehl. "How am I supposed to call up Germany?" said Frau Kahn, "I have no idea
where. I can't just call 'Germany'! We have to know who, we
need to know a telephone number, a person. It's fifty years since
I've spoken German or to a German. Now and then I listen to
the radio, of course, and . . . wait a minute, sometimes they actually give telephone numbers there, 'for your further information'
or for you to call in and play *Say the Magic Word*." Frau Kahn
turned on the radio, tuned to a German station, and left it on
for several hours and we sat there in front of it, listening to the
music and the commercials, the way soldiers listen to battle reports when they're trying to find out who's in trouble where.
All of a sudden Frau Kahn yelled, "Quick, quick, quiet, shhh!"
but you really couldn't hear anything because she kept on
yelling "Quiet, quiet, shhh!" But then they repeated everything
and she was able to get the number down — 07 22 19 20. We
were as excited as if we'd gotten the children back already, as if
I at least had a thread in my hand that I only needed to follow
to the end and then everything would be all right again, and it
would have been just a nightmare in which my husband steals
my children and takes them away, where he's crazy or a criminal. That nightmare, in which I'm suddenly standing there completely alone, and all that's left for me to do is jump off a building
or the bridge over the Rhine.

Frau Kahn mumbled, and then she yelled loudly, "For fifty years! For fifty years!" She started to make telephone calls, in a language I couldn't understand, not a word of it — in German. Everything turned out to be very difficult — they kept on giving her more numbers, then still more, then connected her with other extensions, then transferred her and put her on hold, then transferred her somewhere else, and finally a voice said, "No, we don't make a practice of . . . really, we don't ever . . ." But in the end they did make the announcement for us: "Simon Serfaty is urgently requested to return to home."

"For fifty years" — by that, Frau Kahn meant that she hadn't spoken German for fifty years. Burned all her bridges. Doesn't want to see Germany ever again, hear anything about it, know anything about it, she says. And she doesn't go over to the Aldi Supermarket in Kehl, either, something that most everyone else does. Earlier, I occasionally suggested that we go over and do our shopping there together. No, she didn't want to. Or could I at least bring her a few things, because everything's much cheaper there. No, she wouldn't hear of that, either. Nothing. Never again. The sedative drops she gave me, her cure-all that no one's heard of here? She gets them from Switzerland. She's organized a whole chain of shoppers and shippers that has never broken since 1945 and that sees to it that her medicine cabinet is always full. "I keep hearing about good Germans now," she says. "I certainly never met one. I don't need a thing from them, even if it is cheaper at Aldi. Cannibals!"

Frau Kahn always calls the Germans "cannibals." For a long time I didn't know Frau Kahn's story. Sometimes when I'd bring her mail up from the mailbox, I'd put the magazine *Le Déporté* on the table along with the envelopes and advertisements, and in the summer, if she wore a blouse with short sleeves, you could see the number tattooed on her forearm. Then I realized what had happened. But I never asked her any questions and she never said anything about it. Once we watched a film on television together — it was a bad choice, because it took place during the Nazi era and was about Jewish children who had been hidden at first but were eventually found and deported anyway. Only after the film was over and the commercial was on — I can still see it, a girl was running and jumping on the beach, tossing her blond hair from one side to the other and singing to herself — Frau Kahn started to cry and cried more and more, and then completely broke down in tears. Afterward she told me how she threw her son, still just a tiny baby, over the balcony to her neighbor at the last minute before she was taken away. That was in Belgium. Her husband had already fled to Italy where, at first, he was hidden by the monks in their monastery and later taken by Don Pauli — what a courageous man he was — to the partisans, which is what he wanted. But because of his blond hair and blue eyes, her husband was too conspicuous there in Italy and the cannibals caught him and killed him. Don Pauli had managed to find Frau Kahn after the war and told her everything. "I'll spare you the details, Frau Serfaty," Frau Kahn told me. "Just be glad that things weren't that bad in Algeria." The baby she threw over the balcony was her son Raffael, who's lived in Israel for a long time and comes to see her once or twice a year; much too infrequently, of course, and unfortunately he's not married, either.

Frau Kahn says she doesn't want to talk about it anymore, never again. "But sometimes I have to talk about it anyway and then I can't stop. And then it seems like you'll never be able to talk about anything else at all, because it's the most important thing in the whole world. People would think you're crazy, of course, but you know I'm quite reasonable, a perfectly reasonable neighbor."

I was embarrassed when Frau Kahn cried and told me about those things. I couldn't comfort her — what could I say? I'd often heard similar things from other Ashkenazim — in fact, some of them talk about it all the time, even when you meet them at market, and of course it's in the children's schoolbooks, and even on television there are often films about it, and everything I've seen or heard has turned into a single, huge story in my mind, or even more, into an eerie landscape. A landscape of terror, with Polish and German names — Auschwitz, Warsaw, Treblinka, Nürnberg, Berlin, Dachau — the only names of Polish or German towns I even know, aside from Kehl. But it doesn't keep me from shopping at Aldi, and it's remained just a story. I've never met any of those cannibals in the midst of everyday life, like Frau Kahn has.

"You didn't have things so bad in Africa," the Ashkenazim told us when we came here, but they didn't know very much about how things had really been in Africa. In any case, the Ashkenazim were the elite of suffering, the world champions of martyrdom, and we were real neophytes by comparison, way in the back rows, and besides that half Arab anyway, and we had to start by learning everything — I mean everything — from them.

Between Frau Kahn and me, it's never been important that she's an Ashkenazi and I'm from North Africa. She's not proud and neither am I. We're two women, more or less alone, and so we've joined forces a little. Simon didn't like her from the start.

On the very first day after we'd moved into the building, he invited her over; we should get acquainted, he said. I put out a few dates, figs, and pistachios — which she didn't touch — and then Simon started asking her all sorts of questions about herself and about the other people in the building, and wouldn't stop talking about himself, how he traveled all over the world, all the things he'd seen, how he went to rich people collecting money for Russian or Syrian Jews and for the Yeshivas in Israel.

"And you're a rabbi?" asked Frau Kahn, since "Rabbi Serfaty" was on our front door in big letters. "Yes, of course." Simon started to get mad. Then she wanted to know what kind of a rabbi. "What kind of a rabbi? A rabbi!" She meant where had he been a rabbi, what congregation. "I studied a long time and then I became a rabbi," answered Simon.

"But where?"

"In Singapore."

"In Singapore?"

"I am the Rabbi of Singapore."

Then Frau Kahn laughed out loud — although she's normally shy and restrained — laughed right in his face and Simon threw her out, pushed her out the door and said he didn't ever want to see her again. I told him he should have more respect for the old woman, but he insisted that she should have more respect for him, he was a rabbi. After that, Frau Kahn only came over when he wasn't there, which was more and more often the case. For weeks, months at a time, he didn't come home. But it was already a long time since I'd had any respect for him.

ONE EVENING — it was back in Amiens — there was Simon, standing in front of our door. I was working a lot at the time, day and night duty and on the Christian holidays, of course, Christmas, Easter, New Year's Eve. The other nurses were delighted when I took over their duties and it didn't really matter to me. In return, I was able to take off Rosh Hashanah and Yom Kippur and Passover. Most of the nurses came from every other country imaginable, but we never actually talked about our backgrounds. None of the women ever said anything about her country, her city, her language; I never talked about Oran or Algeria or how we came to France. And yet we were all friends and stuck together because we recognized each other as newcomers, as people who didn't have any deep roots here, who were still having trouble even holding on to the surface of this foreign place.

Back then I thought I'd stay with my mother forever and never marry. In Oran there were always a few old maids that people hadn't been able to marry off and who made the rounds, always having to sit at someone else's table, always just guests.

In fact, there were hardly any men in my life. My father was dead for a long time and I didn't have any brothers. There was only my uncle, back in Oran, who read the weekly lessons with me and my sister every Shabbat afternoon. My cousins were either much too old or much too young for me.

Later, in Amiens, I did go to school with boys and was always falling in love with one of them like the other girls, but that was a secret, of course — Lord help us, who was there to tell it to? But sometimes, maybe at the birthday party of a girlfriend, one of the boys would look at me a little bit, or touch my hand or shoulder when he passed something, and I'd manage to roll that around in my mind for weeks, wondering if it had been love. If my mother had known that there were boys at those birthday parties, she'd never have allowed me to go, not just because there were boys there, but because they were mostly non-Jewish boys. But there were too few Jewish boys in Amiens and I'd know the few there much too long already to be very interested in them or fall in love with them. Most of them married non-Jewish women later or emigrated to Israel.

My sister had it easy, you know, she was pretty and impudent by nature. With her dark eyes and dark curls she was always surrounded by admirers, like Rachel, but with my stringy, ash-blond hair, I felt ugly and pushed back into the corner, like Lea. I was often jealous of her, but later on God did reward me anyway, with six children, like Lea, while my sister only had two, like Rachel.

Elias, who's her husband now, was the brother of her girl-friend from school. She found him quite easily and everything was simple for her and stayed simple — she has all the luck. Right after graduation Elias and my sister got engaged, then married quickly and moved off to Paris. My mother never told Elias, the way Laban told Jacob, that it wasn't customary with us to marry the younger sister before the older one, and so my sister moved away and I stayed there. In the nineteenth arrondissement of Paris they started a kosher catering business. That was a stroke of genius, because it was right at the time when people were beginning to have kosher ceremonies again, circumcisions, Bar Mitzvahs, and weddings. Today there's so much work they can hardly keep their heads above water, and their two sons are already grown and, of course, work with them in their kosher catering business.

My mother had often begged the Rabbi of Amiens — also an Algerian — to find me a husband, from Algeria if possible, but better still, naturally, from Oran. Two or three times young men were introduced to me. We sat around somewhere at someone's table, on the Shabbat or a holiday, the young man on one side with the men and I on the other with the women. We looked at each other now and then, maybe even exchanged a few words after dinner, and then he said he'd call or write, but mostly I never heard from them again.

Only once did I ever see one of those young men again. His name was Yehuda, and every day after his first visit I waited for him to call. Then he sent a postcard, an old view of the city where he lived, on which he'd written, "Greetings, see you soon." I read that card over and over again, like a love letter, until Yehuda finally did spend another Shabbat in Amiens. In the afternoon we took a walk through the city together and then through the park and sat down on a bench, quite close to each other. Yehuda talked and I mostly listened, because, as it was, I could hardly speak from excitement and hope. On the way, we met up with one or another of my mother's friends, of course, and I could imagine the rush they'd be in to tell what they'd just seen — Zohara with Yehuda, hope they'll soon be engaged.

Someone once told me he'd read that being in love was like being crazy. For weeks after that afternoon I really was under a sort of spell in which all I saw was myself on the bench with Yehuda and had only a very distant, hazy awareness of everything else — my mother, my sister, and all the rest of life.

But after that, Yehuda never wrote again — and, as it was, he'd never called — so after several weeks, my delusions about grandiose feelings collapsed and the things and affairs of normal life again took over the spot they'd occupied before the great storm. I already knew that it was all over, even before someone told me that Yehuda had gotten engaged to a girl from Paris. Then I sat at home alone in the evenings with my mother, listening to her complain about her wasted life, about her destroyed family that had been dispersed to the four winds, scattered away to every conceivable city, to Paris, to Tel Aviv, to Montreal, and about her daughter who couldn't find a husband. We quarreled a lot and I cried a lot and thought that my mother shouldn't blame me for everything.

Even then, when he suddenly turned up in front of our door, Simon had white hair and a white beard. He introduced himself and said he was collecting money for the Jews in Russia and the Jews in Syria and for the Yeshivas in Israel where men studied the Torah the entire day. They are the elite of our people and we who are working have to support them, because they need money, a lot of money, and it doesn't just fall from the sky. Other peoples have their elite in the universities where they earn a lot of money and win prizes; but in our case, those who are not studying have to help nourish the elite, give a tenth, for the spirit.

Back then I admired those men and admired Simon for taking such a life upon himself — on the move for weeks at a time, going to strangers to beg, to explain, in order to scrape the money together. "Schnorrer," or "scrounger," is what they're called; that's what Frau Kahn once told me later.

I invited Simon in and brewed peppermint tea; my mother had bought fresh leaves at L'Oriental, imported directly from Morocco. The shop had opened just a few months before and finally we could buy the spices and herbs we needed for our recipes. When Simon smelled the tea, he said, "Ah, a real nar-nar!" Then I knew that he came from an Arab country, too. "Yes, from Morocco," he said, "like the nar-nar."

Truthfully, I have no idea why the Jews ever left there; there wasn't really a war like there was in Algeria where we were, and the country wasn't occupied by the Germans, either, like Tunisia. Naturally Simon started to talk about Mohammed the Fifth right away, just like all the Moroccans — blessed be his memory, how he protected the Jews and all the things he did for them, a brave, good king!

"No, it was because of Israel that we had to leave," said Simon, "because of the war with the Arab countries." He said the blessing before he drank his tea, and even later on he never took a bite without first pronouncing the appropriate blessing. We spoke a little Arabic, then later my mother sat down with us and we talked the whole evening about Oran and Marrakesh — it turned out he had been born and raised in that city — and drank nar-nar made of fresh mint and ate sweet sesame cookies.

I trusted him, his face, his heavy body, and the stories he told all day long about our great rabbis, about Babah Sale from Morocco and Rachbaz from Algeria and Rambam, and even about the Messiah and the time when the Messiah would come to be the savior of Israel and all the nations. Mankind would be relieved of all the burdens of the world, of hunger, sickness, and senseless hatred, and all the nations would recognize our God as the only one. Oh, if only the time were already here! My mother and I sighed like all Jews do when they're on that subject and Simon said he thought the time of the Messiah couldn't be very far off — we didn't have to wait an eternity for him, because it was said that before the arrival of the Messiah, the powers of evil would first gather together and form mountains of wickedness and malevolence. All you had to do was look around. But, of course, we would have to be able to recognize the Messiah; he wouldn't appear in quite the way we expected, with great pomp, worthy of veneration. It is said that he was already here once, or perhaps even more often, in some godforsaken place, in the guise of a schlemiel that everyone laughed at. What? He's supposed to be the one, the biggest good-for-nothing around, who doesn't know anything, can't do anything, and doesn't have anything and is always laughing when we're crying and crying when we're laughing? That dumb boob, that ugly one there, he's supposed to be the one? That's what they said and were simply unable to recognize him, so he turned away again, the Messiah, because it really had been him, the ugly one, the schlemiel, the stupidest one of the bunch.

When I didn't get pregnant right after our marriage and was afraid I might be barren, Simon went with me to Troyes. That's where Rashi, the most learned man of our people, was born and died, and that's where a miracle occurred. In the city there's no mention of any of that, either of Rashi or of the miracle, even though there's a plaque about some unknown general or other on almost every house. The believers know, of course, where the site of the Rashi miracle is located. You turn a few corners in the old city, look around inquiringly, and soon someone will come up or yell out of a window that it's further on, or back there, to the right.

With my uncle, who used to study the weekly lesson with me

and my sister in Oran, we had also read the Rashi scriptures, sentence by sentence, the excerpt first, then Rashi's commentary. It took seven years, because in the first year we read the first of the seven sections of the weekly lessons, then the second one the following year, then the third and so on, until we had gone through the entire Torah. I had always imagined Rashi as one of us, as someone from Oran, one of the famous rabbis whom we revered and in whose name we made promises and wished blessings on each other. Well, it turns out he came from Europe, from one of those cold countries almost on the German border. He'd studied in Germany, Simon told me. He led me into the old city, where the streets are so narrow that two people can hardly even walk side by side, and dark, because the sun is rarely directly overhead. We stopped in front of a piece of wall. I asked what that was, there wasn't really anything to see. But Simon guided my hand across the wall and I noticed that it was uneven, that it bowed inward, and Simon said, "Here it is, this is the place of the miracle, here, where the wall bows inward. A hundred years ago, you see, Rashi's mother was walking along, late in her pregnancy. Suddenly there was a goy with a wagon coming toward her, yelling, 'Hey, make room, get out of the way!' But she could hardly get out of the way, the street was too narrow. The goy screamed, 'All right, don't!' then whipped his horses and was just about to simply gallop right over Rashi's mother with his horses and wagon when she turned toward the wall and implored God for help, not for herself, no, only for her child, and at that moment the wall of the house bulged inward so that she could walk into it and nothing happened to her. Thanks to that miracle, Rashi could be born." Simon had showed me the place and I felt the hollow in the wall with my hands. Shortly afterward I became pregnant with our first daughter whom we named Zippora, like Moses' wife. Our second daughter, who came soon after, we called Elisheva, like Aaron's wife. I dreamed of having many more children with Simon, boys to whom he would teach the Talmud and girls he would instruct in the Torah, using Rashi's commentary, just as my uncle had back in Oran. I'd be busy in the kitchen with my housework and would make peppermint tea and the door would be open, so I could look over at them and hear their voices as they read and translated, and Simon would explain the text to them, patiently and proud of their ambition to learn, and when they were finished he would call out and say, "Zohara, bring the children something sweet, they've studied so hard," and, of course, I would always have a supply of marzipan and candied almonds handy in a little dish.

Simon also thought that our names went well together, Simon and Zohara. On that first evening he talked a lot about the meaning of the names and how they complemented each other: Simon comes from *shama*, in other words, "to hear," and Zohara was like "to see," from "light" or "brightness" as in "the brightness of the firmament," as it says in the book of Daniel: "The teachers shall shine like the brightness of the firmament and all those who have led the multitude in the ways of righteousness." Simon told about the years he'd spent studying the Zohar, the most mysterious and difficult of all of our books, and how he became so excited that he was unable to sleep for nights at a time. And that it would probably be that way again, now that he had met me, Zohara. I blushed. Then he said that the Zohar had been composed among our people, in North Africa, and we Sefardim were not nearly proud enough of our culture. We should not let ourselves be humbled by the Ashkenazim and go around trying to imitate them. That was ridiculous. As if we had completely lost our dignity. "They call us superstitious and uneducated, but the truth is that for all their education they have completely lost their faith. And, for example, a nar–nar like this one here — they know absolutely nothing about it and they can't even prepare a real couscous, let alone a dafina — they have no idea what that is."

We laughed, and even my mother laughed. She gradually lapsed into Arabic during the conversation with Simon, she practically rummaged through her treasure chest of Arabic in order to bring out the finest gems of phrasing and wisdom. And yet she was looking at him rather critically the entire time.

A few weeks later he came visiting again, in the evening; then he even spent a Shabbat with us, and soon he was coming more and more often and, finally, every Friday. At that time, my mother and I of course offered the more extensive Shabbat menu, not the limited one that we prepared for just the two of us. We began as early as Monday to plan for the next Shabbat: which salads, which fish, which soup, which meat, which desserts. So, on Monday we'd think it all over, on Tuesday and Wednesday we'd shop for what we needed, on Thursday we did the pickling and baking, and on Friday we did the cooking. My mother remembered recipes that she used to cook for my father while they were engaged; there were all sorts of secret ingredients and little tricks in order to move things toward marriage, and she gave me a bunch of hints and bits of advice about how to treat a husband and what you should never do or say under any circumstances, as if a husband were like a valuable porcelain plate that could slip out of your hands and be smashed forever if you weren't careful. I said to my mother, "But if we love each other, things will be all right without making such a fuss."

ONLY ONCE DID I ever go on a long trip. From Algeria to France. A trip from which I never returned. I didn't actually experience the Algerian War very much, just heard shots in the distance during the evening or at night, when it was quiet otherwise; but we could only move around in areas that became more and more limited from week to week; don't go there any more, not there either — every morning our mother laid out new boundaries for my sister and me, so that we wouldn't go walking into a crossfire or some other horrible thing. Every day another girl, sometimes two, would be missing from school. They'd gone away with their parents, left Algeria, and they didn't let on to anyone about it beforehand. It was dangerous to just take off like that; the outcome of the war wasn't clear yet and the OAS was threatening anyone who gave up on Algeria voluntarily. Despite that, the classrooms were emptying out and the apartment houses were getting to be empty as well. Every day there was a new surprise. Oh, them? They're gone, and they are, too. But it was really better not to talk about it anymore, out of fear. Then one day the war was over, and our life in Algeria was over as well. We sat around with I don't know how many thousand others in temporary camps on the edge of the sea and waited for a place on a ship — my mother, my sister, and I. Two suitcases were all we had with us; you couldn't take more. Both of them were stuffed mainly with bags and cans in which my mother had brought all sorts of spices that were absolutely essential to our cooking, since she rightly assumed we wouldn't be able to find them easily in Europe. "If nowhere else," mother often said later, "at least we can rediscover the smells and tastes of Oran in our kitchen."

On the day before we sailed, mother went with us to father's grave, so that we could say goodbye to him, to him and our grandparents and all our other ancestors who were lying there together in the cemetery. Beside the cemetery, right next to it, they say there's a new housing complex. For a long time the "former residents" of Oran have been collecting money and sending it over to pay for the upkeep of the cemetery, and they claim it's still in more or less passable condition and not plowed under the way they are in other countries, thank God.

Then one day we were standing on the deck of a big ship that was casting off from the coast and everyone was crying, all the children, all the women, and most of the men, too. That was a different goodbye than usual. Not just for a brief separation, for a vacation, for a few days or weeks. This time it was goodbye to everything, to a whole country — forever. We'd lived there for two thousand years! Sixty generations! Not just for a ridiculous three or four like the French who threw it all away. Everyone was sighing, wailing, lamenting, "We're the last of so many generations. The last of all. What a tragedy! What's going to happen next?"

When nothing more could be seen but the sea, an indifferent, gray sea, everyone went in from the deck and then it was very quiet on the ship for three whole days, as if the passengers had fallen into a deep sleep. They only emerged from it when the opposite shore of the Mediterranean became visible — the coast of France. Most of the people hoped they'd be able to stay right there, on the coast, in Marseille or Nice, at least at the edge of the sea on whose other shore lay the country they'd left, as if you weren't so completely cut off and could still say, "Oceans do not separate us, oceans bind us together" However, only a few managed to settle in the cities there, only those who already had a brother, a cousin, or an in-law there who could take them in and help them get started. Instead, we got sent to Amiens. There, after we'd spent days in a camp again, we were divided up and settled in a former chocolate factory, ten women to a room. It was October and the cold weather started right away, with the darkness and the long twilight hours of unending indecision between light and dark, when the day dies such a painful death, not quick and easy as it was back home. "As neatly as with the guillotine," my uncle once said. Soon winter came and we had no winter coats or heavy clothing, no warm shoes or boots. Of course, we never needed them in Oran. And the sea was no longer there, and nothing else that we were used to. Every square, every street, every tree, every house, and every person was new.

The former Algerians stuck together, but they all came from very different parts of the country, and it's hard to imagine how big the differences are between people from the various areas, not to mention those from the Sahara.

In the Jewish community there was no one else from Oran. My mother made friends with women from other Algerian cities; they exchanged memories and complained and told each other about all the things they'd had to leave back there, their homes, their businesses, and the graves of their parents. "Can you imagine, after we've lived there for two thousand years, kicked out like dogs! After two thousand years!" It wasn't that they missed their "homeland," but their houses, their gardens, the sea, the beach, the mild climate and a different way of living — an easier, more tolerant one, as they put it.

At first mother cried all the time, as soon as she'd gotten up in the morning and when she went back into bed at night, and during the night as well. She couldn't stop crying. She cried for three years and I have no memories of her from that time without her sobbing, sniffling, wiping tears away — draped across the table with her head in her arms, bawling, year after year.

Maybe others were luckier, adapted more easily, found a better job more quickly, got used to the new situation more easily. Perhaps they'd also realized earlier that the time in Algeria was over and had been preparing themselves — at least in their minds — for a new life in another country. If our father had still been living, he would have been given a new job right away, since he was a railroad employee, but my mother had never really worked, and lived on a small pension. But that wasn't the worst thing. The worst thing was that she didn't know what to do with herself all day, there was no one to visit or talk with or for whom she could cook, bake, or prepare a celebration; the whole family had been torn apart and scattered to every city imaginable; some had even ended up in Canada.

In Oran, when our father was still living, how many people had sat around the table in our apartment on Friday evenings? The entire clan — uncles, aunts, and countless boy and girl cousins — everyone lived in everyone else's home so to speak, and everyone was always visiting everyone else; there was no such thing as a closed door or keeping to yourself — what was the point of that, anyway? The women lived in a more or less isolated world, of course, like a parliament that was constantly in session, where there were always a great many urgent matters to discuss, advise about, and decide, and where nothing new could remain a secret or go without comment.

My sister and I tried to put an end to all that. We told our mother that we wanted to start a new life, there in Amiens — why did you bother always talking about France with so much respect and love — a civilized country! A free country! You have equal rights with everyone else and even have French passports! So just stop your crying, just stop it once and for all!

We wanted to make friends with other girls from Amiens, meet them after school, or go to the movies with them. But mother never permitted it. She never permitted anything — we weren't allowed to go to the movies or the park, and certainly not visiting. She was afraid to even let us out of her sight. At that time, just like our girlfriends, we were collecting postcards with pictures of actors and we sent them away and got autographs. We hadn't seen the films, of course, but we'd at least looked at the stills in the advertisements outside the theater and our friends had told us all about them. But when mother found our collection, she threw it out, just the way she'd thrown everything else away, all the things that in her eyes served no purpose and so were useless and senseless. There was nothing in our apartment that was more than three years old. She said she didn't want to get attached to anything anymore and didn't want to go collecting any new mementos that you'd just have to throw overboard again and watch everything sink to the bottom, irretrievably.

Mother died just last year and I cried for a long time, even though I'm over forty and have six children. Thank God she didn't die in the hospital, but at my sister's house, where she lived for the last several years after she got to the point where she couldn't take care of herself any longer. She had difficulty reading and writing for all of her life and she never did learn to speak French without making mistakes. For that reason alone either I or my sister had to be near her all the time, to go with her to the doctor, for instance, because, although she could recognize a doctor's name plate, there were often several of them in a row and they all looked the same — pediatrician, eye doctor, cardiologist — and you had to drop her off at the right one, at least the first time.

Ever since she'd come across to Europe, her heartbeat got slower and slower and weaker and weaker. She was no longer able to lead a normal life and spent the rest of her days just waiting for the end, laying down age-rings like a tree, motionlessly. She looked into herself or stared out of the window, as if she could find her lost, mourned homeland again within herself or outside beyond the window. Her heart attacks came like outbursts of rage against the unjustness of fate and the Arabs, who'd robbed her, deceived her, and driven her out, although people had actually been on friendly terms — distant, but friendly. And eventually the Arabs had asked for advice and blessings from our rabbis and called our doctors when they got sick. And we'd lived there before them, for centuries in fact, before the Arabs from who knows where invaded the country.

Mother just faded away slowly. I could see that when I visited her in the summer, year after year, at my sister's, where we all spent our long vacations together. My sister's house is located on the edge of Paris and has a lot of room for the children, a fairly big garden in which they can run around, and, as the biggest attraction, Billy the dog, whom they pull around and try to teach tricks, which, of course, he never learns. At home there are pictures of him pinned all over the walls — Billy sleeping, Billy eating, Billy sniffing at something, Billy sitting in the garden.

Shortly before my mother died, I took her to the doctor in their suburb, after she'd complained about her heart all night long. The doctor said he'd take an EKG, so would she undress and lie down on the examining table. I had to help her, because she was so weak, but gradually we managed to peel off her clothes. I had never seen her naked before in my whole life and turned my head away. She said, "Please, stay with me." She was more afraid of dying than ashamed and suddenly it was as if we had exchanged roles and I was the mother and she was my child and that thought repelled me even more; even if I was going to nurse her during her illness the way I'd already nursed a lot of people in the hospital, I just didn't want everything to be turned around so suddenly.

My mother was always extremely modest and closed her door or wrapped herself up in front of my sister and me. There was always a lingering smell of her eau de cologne that drifted through the apartment like the Sahara breeze. It was Je Reviens, by Worth — I still see it sometimes today, the perfectly round bottle with the little angel sitting on it with crossed legs. I even try some now and then, and the saleswomen always ask whether it's for an older lady, because there's not much call for it anymore and it's been out of fashion for a long time, and I say, "Yes, yes, it's for an older lady."

During the last weeks before her death, our mother was only able to get around by taking tiny, little steps — at first just around the neighborhood, then only a few streets away, then just in front of the house, then only in the garden, eventually not even out of the house and then not even out of her room, and finally not even out of bed. My sister said to me on the phone that she was "halfway there, you know." And one morning she found her dead, covered with her woolen blanket, the television still turned on from the night before.

During the week of mourning my sister's kosher catering service was closed. Elias could have run the business alone, of course, but the two of them are such a practiced team that one probably couldn't get along without the other. We sat on the floor with our torn clothing and a few friends and acquaintances of mother's came by — the old-timers from Oran or somewhere else in Algeria, and once again they dragged out their memories of days gone by — the city, the sea, the crossing. Conversations are always difficult during the period of mourning because the funeral guests belong to the living, but for a time the mourners belong more to the dead, or at least to a world in between; they aren't able to speak and feel the way they did just a few days before, when they belonged entirely to the living — that world has suddenly become foreign to them.

But some people react to them in a different way, with a look of mutual understanding, of shared experience, as if the mourner were being accepted into some secret society — those who no longer have any parents and, in the succession of the generations, have moved up into the front line where there's no longer any protection.

Sometimes when I'm walking along the street and happen to catch a glance of my reflection in a display window, I see my mother more and more often instead of myself, and I ask myself whether I'm soon going to turn into her entirely — my face, my body, my being. Because I sense this change in my stride, in my movements, in my look, I hear myself speaking with my mother's voice, and I see myself gesturing with her hands, "Oh, no! Oh dear, oh God save us!"

I WOKE UP AT half past six in the morning, just as I did every other day, lying alone in our room; the children's beds were empty. Six flat, smooth, empty beds were standing there as if they'd never been used. It seemed as if I'd awakened on another planet — a planet circling around in a mute universe without life. Usually when I open my eyes in the morning our planet is already vibrating with commotion, screaming, quarreling, and carrying on. Zippora can't find her things, suspects that one of the boys has taken them, and is yelling at all three of them. Elisheva, on the other hand, hasn't gotten out of bed — she does everything so slowly — and now I'm the one who's yelling for her to finally get a move on. Ruth is arguing with Jonathan, and Daniel and Michael are seeing who can scream the loudest. The whole room is in an uproar with all the yelling and running back and forth and jumping up and down on the beds.

Now, however, it was completely quiet in the apartment. There wasn't a single sound. For the first time, I even heard noises from the neighbors' apartments — a telephone ringing, a washing machine rumbling, a woman's voice, a man's voice, loud coughing — even though the building had pretty well emptied out over the last few days; from the window I'd already seen several of the neighbors loading their bags into their cars and driving off for vacation.

I lay there rigidly; I couldn't even move for fear of being set out on that dead planet and having to survive somehow. See how you're going to figure that out! The whole apartment seemed to be stuffed full of emptiness, silence, and loneliness like gigantic blocks of stone, boulders, mountains. How was I even going to make it through a single day in that petrified isolation, without anything to keep me busy? Before, I was always doing something with the children, everything in my life revolved solely around my children. Most of the time there's more than I can do, more commotion, noise, and carrying on than I can bear. It's that way especially in the morning, and when I've finally gotten them all out of their beds, washed and dressed, I still have to run around looking for this and that, whatever they need, getting everything imaginable out, packed together, tied up. Everyone's standing in someone else's way and there's no room for the shoe rack anywhere but on the balcony outside the kitchen, where we're finally sitting down to eat when someone goes running out, leaving the door open so the others feel the draft — and someone always has a cold as it is — and I scream "Close the door!" and go on with the rest of the litany: *stop that, leave it alone, hurry up, why are you arguing again already, now that'll do, okay that's it!*

I called Dr. Schwab. I actually felt sick, sick all over, pains everywhere — in my neck, in my back, in my belly. My muscles hurt and my skin burned. I couldn't even get up because of it all. Dr. Schwab needed to come, at least someone needed to take a look at me, listen to me, worry about me — someone to whom I could say that I didn't feel well without having to be ashamed of myself. Of course, I didn't tell him what had happened, although he certainly must have wondered why not one of the children was at home in the middle of vacation. It wasn't long since he'd sewed up Jonathan on the kitchen table. Jonathan had gotten out of the bathtub with wet feet and went chasing around the apartment after Ruth, who'd once again done some dumb thing to annoy him, and then he managed to fall and hit his forehead against a sharp edge in the hallway. So much blood poured out of the wound that I called Dr. Schwab right away in a panic. He put Jonathan on the kitchen table and we had to hold him while Dr. Schwab sewed up the cut with three stitches. It was all over quickly but Zippora and Elisheva — who were actually supposed to be helping — screamed so much that Dr. Schwab threw them out of the kitchen.

Now he was saying, "There's really nothing wrong with you Mrs. Serfaty, at least not physically — perhaps you just need a good rest." He prescribed magnesium as a tonic and gave me the slip for the insurance, and then left.

As soon as he was out of the door, the clumps of emptiness took over the entire apartment again and the silence wrapped itself around every piece of furniture, around every chair, around every table. So I started to move things and push them back and forth, in order to set them free and keep myself from being crushed and to make a survival corridor for myself. Then I started to do the wash, anything that was still in the closets, mainly winter things, of course, because I'd packed the summer things for the children — the dresses, shorts, T-shirts, and sandals. I took the anoraks and thick sweaters out of the drawers and closets and washed them — first the red things, then the blue ones, then the light-colored things — and hung them up on the balcony. With the heat, everything dried quite rapidly and in a few hours I was able to take the anoraks, sweaters, and wool stockings off the line again; then I ironed and folded each piece and put it back in the closet. Next I took on the winter quilts, the sheets, and the towels. For at least three days I was beside myself, washing, drying, ironing, putting away, from morning until it got dark at night around ten. At the same time, I was constantly hovering around the telephone, listening to hear if it was ringing, and running to the mailbox to see if there was a letter, expecting that, any minute, someone would be bringing me news, and I must have yanked the apartment door open a hundred times because I thought I heard knocking or voices in the corridor, the voices of Zippora and Elisheva and Ruth and the voices of Daniel and Michael and little Jonathan. But it was pointless — each time all I did was gape into the dark hole of the corridor, horrified.

In between washing and ironing I prayed the Psalms, the way we did back then, on the ship from Oran: "And I am poor and wretched, my God, care for me. My help is with You, You are my savior. My God, do not delay." I prayed to God only for the return of my children, nothing else. It had been a long time since I cared what happened to Simon. He should just let me and my children live in peace.

So that the line wasn't busy at the very moment my children might call, I didn't use the phone myself and didn't even go out of the house for fear of missing that moment. I ate things that were in the deep freeze. There's always plenty in the house. I just grabbed something out of a plastic container — frozen leftovers from a previous meal — that I warmed up, and as I stood in front of the stove at noontime and stirred my pot, the clattering of plates, the clink of knives and forks, and the scraping of chairs echoed from the windows that opened onto the courtyard and it was as if the whole city were sitting down at one big table simultaneously, but I was excluded and had to eat from my bowl alone, like a dog.

Of course the other reason I didn't leave the house was to avoid meeting people. At the market, for instance, I'm always running into women I know and you stand there talking and soon someone else comes along. Other than on the Shabbat, at the synagogue, that's really the only opportunity I have to meet people, because I almost never get an invitation — who's going to invite a woman with six children? But if I were to meet some-one now, it would be natural for them to ask "How are you? What're the children doing?" And what would I say then? That they're not even here, they've been kidnapped by their father, I have no idea where, or for how long, and I don't even know why?

It was already hard enough to explain where my husband was all those years — on a trip, on the road somewhere, collecting donations. People looked at me sympathetically and later the time came when we all acted as if we'd already forgotten him, as if he didn't even exist, at least not in the present.

After washing I started on the housecleaning, moved all the furniture out and pushed it together and then scrubbed and rinsed and vacuumed the way I usually only do before Pesach and didn't miss a crack or corner in the whole apartment. Last of all I went after the bedroom. Each of the children has a little chest beside the bed and a small shelf on the wall where they keep things that belong just to them "and nobody else," as they sometimes say. Things that belong to all of them together are kept in boxes under the beds. First I dusted the outside of every-thing and then opened the drawers to wipe them out and lying there was whatever each child had just tossed in: notebooks from school, pens and pencils, pieces of things they wrote, drawings, half-finished designs, and all sorts of little booklets, little pictures, and junk. Each of the children had left there a sort of life's work that now seemed broken off and incomplete. I picked up each object individually and then carefully put it back in the place it had been assigned according to some plan — one that I didn't understand, but which I now respected, and I realized that I thought of my children too little as individuals and much too often as just a noisy flock. Sometimes I can't even tell them apart on baby pictures and have to try to figure out which one was how old in which apartment.

The big box with the Lego pieces is kept under Daniel's bed; I pulled it out and put it on the bed in order to wipe the floor, then I rummaged around a bit in the Legos and picked out a couple of the little men, then set up a little crew of Lego men, and finally I just turned the box over and emptied it out. With a huge clatter, a mountain of Lego pieces grew up in the space between the children's beds and I sat down beside it and started to sort the pieces: twos, fours, sixes, wheels, windows, doors, black ones, blue ones, red, yellow, white — green ones were few and far between. Then I started to build, setting the side walls around a big area, one above the other, higher and higher; it was getting to be something like a house, but since I'd forgotten the windows, my structure actually looked more like a ship. So I built a ship — there were certainly enough masts and ladders and even a few treasure chests that I stowed below deck; then I put in all sorts of animals and the crew that I'd set up first; and then I realized that I'd built myself an ark, like Noah. Now I, too, had to barricade myself in and wait for the end of this flood of misfortune that had inundated me, until the wind came up and the waters receded again.

I waited, went on waiting, went on washing, cleaning, dust-ing. The days dropped away, ran away, the telephone seemed out of order, totally mute, the mailbox stayed empty, no one knocked, the doorbell didn't ring, no one was standing in front of my door. I reminded myself of a leftover piece of meat that was starting to spoil.

H OW DID SIMON even get to Singapore? When you come right down to it, I didn't know a thing about his life. All he ever told me were stories and legends. Legends about saints and scholars and stories about the simple and wonderful life in Morocco, where one was still respected and had a whole flock of servants. And otherwise, what I heard mostly was, "The Talmud says," and "The Gemarah says," "Shulchan Aruch says," as if his life took place only in legendary times or in the rituals of the books.

Actually, his name was Abraham, like all Moroccans. That I discovered by chance in his passport. Then he took to calling himself Simon and it was by that name I got to know him. I didn't know what that change of names meant, but maybe it should have given me a hint. Simon had sometimes said that he belonged to the one tribe that didn't receive a blessing from Moses in the days before his death. The way he said it was as if an injustice had been done to him personally and he'd get upset about it, as if it had actually played a role in his life. Then I'd say, "My God, that's just an old story, nobody thinks about it anymore," but he'd get more and more worked up about it and insist that it had been an injustice.

My mother had given me lots of good advice about my marriage: you have to subordinate yourself to your husband, adjust to his personality, not ask too much, not upset him with your little problems, and show him that you admire him as well — do a little bit of acting. "But that's awful," I said. And she said, "Well, yes, it's awful, but that's the way it is."

Every time I had a child, Simon became more unfriendly toward me. In the beginning I thought it was because the first three children were girls and he wanted a boy. Then, when I finally had a boy, I wanted to call him Levi just like Lea did, because she hoped that then Jacob would finally feel more closely tied to her. But Simon claimed, "No one has Levi for a first name nowadays! Our first son is going to be named Daniel, with the legal name of Jean-Jacques."

Each of our children was born in a different city, because we kept having to move, God knows why. Just when I'd gotten myself half settled in a city and was beginning to find my way around a bit and had done a little exploring in my territory — the boundaries of which were staked out pretty narrowly as it was — or had met this or that person and perhaps had even met them more than once, everything had to be broken off again, in a panic that was inexplicable to me, and then things went on in the same way again, another move to another city.

I never got beyond the boundaries of my territory in any of those cities, never learned anything more about them than the way to schools, kindergartens, the doctor's, the drug store, the market, the synagogue, and the kosher butcher, and I never saw any of the sights or the center of the city, and certainly not the suburbs or surrounding countryside. The variation in the climates of those cities that differed so little from each other was something I only noticed by how quickly or slowly the wash dried on the balcony. Except that in Nantes it never really dried at all, because it never stopped raining there. That was the city I found easiest to leave.

If there was a park in my neighborhood, we sometimes went walking there on the Shabbat, and I'd sit on a bench while the children played, watching them and thinking about why Simon changed his name and why he had to lead such an unsettled life and drag me all around with him. But I never found an answer to those questions and just got used to things and thought we all had our own fates: some people got shaken up by an earthquake or some other horrible event caught up with them — our history is full of that — and back then, when we had to leave Algeria so suddenly, I didn't understand why, either. So I often thought I was like the mechanical toy dog that the children played with sometimes — he goes and goes, but then suddenly that's it, he falls over on his nose — the batteries have run out. When he's running around, the children put an obstacle in his way — an apple or a book — which he can actually avoid. At first he bumps up against it a couple of times, then he goes around it. For years, that dog was the only toy the children owned and we had to keep it hidden from Simon — he wouldn't allow dolls or animals because they suggested idols, and, of course, no picture books or comics, either, because images were forbidden. In general the children were supposed to come in contact only with sacred things. He went snuffling through their school books for forbidden subjects like the origin of the world or the evolutionary theory of human life and, of course, for forbidden illustrations of naked people in their biology or art books. The children then had to paste those pages together under his supervision. He called up the teachers who were responsible for that disgraceful situation and yelled at them the way he yelled at us, which was about the only way he spoke to us at all, because most of the time he sat at his desk reading the holy books and we had to go on tiptoe so as not to disturb him. But the knowledge that he obtained from those books he kept to himself; he didn't study the Talmud with the boys or the Torah with the girls — all he did was snap at them, because nothing that happened in our home was right as far as he was concerned. He accused me of letting up on the reins when it came to the children's upbringing, which one could easily see by the getups they ran around in — the girls' skirts were much too short and the sleeves of their blouses weren't long enough, either, and the boys — just like the goyim.

Once — I no longer have any idea in which city it was — he surprised me as I was using the table to change a diaper on Michael, our youngest at that point, because my back hurt from constantly changing him on the bed. We didn't own a changing table, of course, because we hardly owned anything at all, since Simon earned almost nothing or at least acted as if he didn't keep any of the money he collected, and I'd stopped working in the hospital after the third child. We lived on the allotment for children and the housing allowance — in other words, on welfare from the state; what Simon lived on during his more and more frequent and ever-longer trips I never knew and never asked.

When he saw me changing the child on the table, he yelled at me and asked me if I'd gone completely crazy — that was, after all, the table at which he read the holy scriptures, did I want to profane the spot with kids' behinds and diapers? I was barely able to grab the little one before he was already sweeping everything off the table — baby oil, baby cream, and diapers — and then he knocked over the table, ran into the kitchen, grabbed a hammer, and began to demolish the table, hacking and pound-

ing away at it and tearing it apart until nothing was left but a pile
of wood, which he carried downstairs to the courtyard and
threw in with the trash — a brand-new table. It was one of the
very few purchases that we'd ever been able to afford. We'd gone
to the furniture store where they were having their "Discount
Week," and argued over every piece we looked at. If I said it was
something we needed, Simon said we didn't need it; if I said I
liked it, he said he didn't like it. Only when we came to the table
did we agree right away that we needed it and that we liked it.
But when I hesitated because of the price, Simon pointed out
that it wasn't a matter of a purchase, but of an investment. Since
we'd be using the table for sacred purposes — the Shabbat meals
and the studies — some day we'd get our expense back two or
three times over. The Eternal One would see to it. And that's the
table Simon threw in the trash.

Earlier, I'd believed everything he said. I'd admired him and
looked upon him as a holy man; I was entranced by his white
beard and the blessings he pronounced at every opportunity and
was enchanted by his stories. Sometimes I'd ask him why this
was forbidden and that permitted, but he never gave me an
answer to any of the questions. Only slowly did I begin to doubt
what he said and did, then stopped believing his speeches and
lecturing, and eventually I didn't even listen to him and finally I
became suspicious about all the other business — his trips and
collecting donations. Perhaps he felt as if I'd seen through him;
at any rate, he came home less and less frequently and eventually
not at all and then we only met at the railroad station in Kehl
where he'd start lecturing us again and finding fault with everything under the sun and end up by repeating the whole thing,
how I was incapable of being educated in any way and how did
I think the children were going to turn out and that I didn't
need to be surprised if they all married goyim some day.

The longer Simon was away, and the more infrequently he reappeared after his journeys, the less we spoke of him; sometimes I even thought that perhaps the children had actually forgotten him already, but it was more likely an unspoken agreement between us that we'd act as if we had gotten completely accustomed to having to live pretty much on our own and were basically happy about that or at least relieved. I learned to manage by myself. The pressing problems and important decisions for the year I discussed with my sister and her husband when we spent the summer at their place and the children were wandering through the gardens with Billy.

After the summer vacations, my brother-in-law usually drove us back to Strasbourg in his car, the trunk crammed with toys, books, and comics for the children. Once my sister even picked up a television set that was lying around broken, but after Elias had pounded on it and adjusted a few things and tightened a few screws, it worked fine in our apartment for several years. We made a place for it by pushing a few holy books off to one side.

At the beginning of our life together, at least Simon and I still argued sometimes. I soon discovered that it wasn't love that kept us together, but I really did hope for a sort of being pleased with one another, the kind of sticking together and working together I saw with my sister and her husband. But soon Simon was living in a way that was turned away from me completely, as if he didn't want to see or hear anything of me at all, as if his life revolved around something completely different; he didn't listen to me, didn't ask me anything, never gave me a chance to say a thing or utter a thought, and in all those years he never once said to me, "You're right."

Now it seems to me as if, in the midst of the endless moving here and there and the constant packing and unpacking, we'd lost, one by one, the suitcases that we'd intended to carry together. In the beginning I still tried desperately to find one or another of them, but I soon realized that they were of no value to Simon, things he just kept knocking out of my hand over and over. And so, with time, everything was lost: at first admiration and respect, then tenderness and the hope of finding security with Simon, and, later, friendship — that sort of trust and familiarity that arises when people live together under one roof — until, finally, he became something that was more like an enemy to me. As if that awful proverb that I heard in Oran had come true: "Remember, you do not marry your father, nor your brother, but your enemy."

The last time we stood with Simon at the station in Kehl, I told him to his face what I'd been thinking for a long time. While the children were paging through Mickey Mouse comics at the magazine stand, I said to him, "Simon, I think you're a fraud." He answered by cursing at me in Arabic and ran up the stairs to the platform in a rage and then we didn't hear a thing from him for a long time, even longer than usual. But when he called and said he wanted to go on vacation with us, I thought maybe we could talk to each other now and that he'd explain everything to me. That maybe, as they say, we could still make a fresh start.

I'D SET ALL MY hopes on the Shabbat. At least Simon would call on Friday and let me talk to the children, I thought. And if he'd gone completely crazy, maybe he'd even call on the Shabbat itself, though it's forbidden. I didn't unplug the telephone as I always did on Fridays just before the start of the Shabbat, and I would even have answered the telephone if it had rung, just to hear my children's voices again and to find out what had actually happened and when this nightmare would end. I would have used the telephone on the Shabbat even though it's forbidden, and God wouldn't have held it against me because he's probably on my side in this affair. And anyway, it's not a real Shabbat without children. Without family, the Shabbat loses all meaning. In Oran, even those who were unmarried or widowed didn't have to be alone, but found a place around the tables of their families. To be by yourself on the Shabbat is like a wedding at which the bride doesn't appear. But where was I supposed to go, and who was going to invite me, since no one knew anything about my troubles? And I didn't want to tell anyone about it — I was just too ashamed.

Usually I start with the preparations by nine in the morning on Friday, and even when the Shabbat doesn't begin until late in the evening in the summertime, I push myself all day long and by evening I'm completely done in — I whirl around like a lunatic and yet I still don't know how I'm ever going to get done in time. First thing in the morning I start on the breads, and while the dough is rising I go to the market. Then come the preparations for the dafina, cleaning the vegetables, shelling them, cutting them up, and inspecting them for those small, forbidden creatures, turning every leaf, because they creep under the leaves and into the smallest sprouts and hide. Then everything goes onto the stove to get cooked. And there's still the cake to bake. In Oran, no woman ever stood in her kitchen alone — everyone had two or three Arab women to help. They were called "fatmas" and lived in the house with us and did everything — the cooking, the cleaning, taking care of the children. They were just part of the clan. Even earlier they were called slaves, but they were treated well, according to the precepts of our religion.

About two in the afternoon the children come home from school, make a mess of everything, want something to eat right away, and get into the refrigerator. At least Zippora and Elisheva help a little by cleaning up the living room and vacuuming, but the boys just stand around and get in the way, and the closer we get to evening the more there's left to do, and we're snatched up by a tornado whose center, naturally, is the kitchen, but at a certain moment it moves over to the bathroom, because we all still have to get into the shower. I send the first child out of the shower — usually Zippora, who's the fastest at everything — for the newspaper, which we buy only on Fridays because of the television schedule, and then the tornado works itself up to one

last climax of racing past each other, sliding out of each other's
way, looking for things, getting them mixed up, back and forth
between bathroom, kitchen, and closets, the laundry pile and
the clean clothes; and when I finally light the candles and we're
all sitting at the table eating, it's like a gigantic sigh, then the six
days of the week and all the turmoil fall away from me and the
Shabbat actually comes into our apartment and I can sense how
my second soul enters me, how equanimity and a huge sense of
well-being spread over me. After we've eaten, I settle into one
of the easy chairs, leaving all the dishes, plates, and leftovers on
the table, and I don't lift a finger to do another thing, and I
teach the children that you don't always have to get everything
done right away, because it'll keep until tomorrow. Otherwise it
might turn out that that evening was the last evening of all, and
if there was nothing left to be done, you could just go ahead and
die right away. At least that's what they used to say in Oran.
Then I can finally read the TV guide in peace and look at the
programs for the coming week, even though I almost never
watch television, because during the week I usually go to bed
at the same time as the children. Only at suppertime do we turn
on the television; around a quarter to seven there's an American
serial about a rich family that takes place in a mansion with a
huge garden and several dogs, all twice as big as Billy. The family members play tennis, ride horses, lead a luxurious life, and
still aren't happy, there are always arguments and misunderstandings, deceit, lies — much worse than it is with us, but the
problems get solved more quickly than they do here, probably
because they have to be done by half past seven. After that we
sometimes watch *Knock, Knock, Who's There?* on channel 1 or
May the Best Man Win on channel 2, mainly in order to divide
up the winnings among ourselves. Daniel and Michael take the
ski and scuba equipment, Zippora and Elisheva the electronic

gadgets, Jonathan and Ruth quarrel over the big, stuffed animals, and I take the weekend at EuroDisney and tell the children I'm going there alone for a little peace and quiet and all they're going to get is a postcard from me. But on Friday evenings, the children actually do leave me in peace for the most part — they respect my second soul and quarrel a little less, or at least a bit more quietly, and they even bring my coffee over to the easy chair. But despite the coffee, I soon fall asleep without any trouble, without counting butterflies. The children wake me around eleven and say, "Mama, come to bed!"

When the doorbell rang at three o'clock on that Friday afternoon, I could feel my heart beating in my throat. But there was Frau Kahn standing in front of the door, asking what I was doing that evening. "We could eat together," she said. "I'll cook the fish and you can make a dafina."

Only as I was cleaning the vegetables did I begin to wonder how Frau Kahn got such an idea and how she even realized that it was Friday, because she really never notices whether it's Tuesday, Wednesday, or the Shabbat. She says she's an atheist, a Jew who doesn't believe in God, or, let's say, doesn't believe any longer.

Dafina with potatoes and leeks, olives, chickpeas, and a lot of oil and meat — that's what I've eaten every Shabbat of my entire life, in France, in Oran; and only during the weeks in the chocolate factory in Amiens was there a lapse — then we had to make do with canned tuna fish and olives out of a bottle. "Austerity Shabbat," is what my sister and I called it back then. Frau Kahn was really right when she said I should prepare a dafina — what was I supposed to do, starve to death?

We live on the very same floor and one of us comes from Mannheim and the other from Oran. "Two places that could hardly be farther away from one another," said Frau Kahn. "Now we live here, not because we picked out this city or this country, but because they threw us out of the places we come from and neither of us can go back again. Not you and not me, not to Mannheim and not to Oran."

Of course we could travel there, take a trip on the train or by boat, or go by car. We could step out and let them think we were visitors, people who stroll through the cities of the world, take a quick look, and write a few postcards. But we wouldn't be able to disguise ourselves and would secretly still go looking for our streets, our apartments, and the old names; and somebody there, someone who lives there and doesn't know us from Adam, would notice us, maybe, and watch us and ask "Are you looking for something here, can I help you?" We'd answer, "Thanks, no, it's okay," because we wouldn't want to let ourselves be caught and, besides, we'd know that the truth was that it had all evaporated into thin air, just the way we ourselves had.

"How often does a person ever find firm ground again, Frau Serfaty?" said Frau Kahn. "And believe you me, people who've lived in a place for a long time can never understand refugees."

She'd made a sort of gefilte fish, the second holiest of holies for the Ashkenazim after the concentration camps. You can hardly even talk about it with them. It seems like the Ashkenazim put sugar on everything they eat, even meat and fish. They learned that from the Poles, who are their worst enemies otherwise, yet at the same time they talk about Warsaw like they do about Jerusalem and all of them have a map of the city in their heads.

"I'm from Germany, Frau Serfaty. Not all Ashkenazim come from Poland, as you might think," Frau Kahn let me know, as she often had already. "Mannheim, that's not even two hours from here by train. I could show you the street where my parents had their lingerie shop, right in the center of the city. My parents were German or, let's say, they and their friends wanted to be German and modern, and the shop was even open on Saturday, of course. There really wasn't much left of God and his laws. But then the modern Germans took off their disguises and turned out to be cannibals, and rounded up my parents and their friends in broad daylight, in the center of the city — I could show you that place, too — and took them to that camp. Those of us who were young at the time fled to other countries, but they even came looking for us in the other countries, the way cannibals go looking for human flesh."

Frau Kahn always says "those camps" and "the cannibals." She's invented a separate language for "that," because you can't, as she says, describe "it." Some who have experienced "that" now go from school to school telling about it, they write books and publish them and have transformed "it" into a story you can tell and that they probably even have to go on telling without stopping. "I could never do that," she says. "I've found my niche in the 'Cercle Vladimir Rabi' — we're atheists, not a congregation, we just get together. We meet now and then, we discuss things, we remember, we do some research, and listen to lectures. Pilgrimages to former concentration camps are on the agenda too, of course — we take flowers, plant trees, mourn, and sometimes meet Christians who are also bringing flowers and planting trees and mourning. I only made the pilgrimage a single time. It was a big convention and we came together from every conceivable country. Just imagine — an entire hotel off in the provinces, full of former concentration camp inmates who are seeing each other for the first time in years and, of course, are yelling to each other, running around, screaming, howling, and even fainting! The hotel people had more or less fled the scene and left us on our own. As soon as we set foot in 'our' concentration camp again, some people had epileptic seizures or other sorts of attacks. That trip took me back twenty years and Raffael had to put me in the hospital for a few weeks afterward.

"I go to the synagogue whenever I'm invited to one of those countless Bar Mitzvahs, engagements, or weddings that this city never seems to lack, and that's already enough for me — I can't summon up any more religious feeling than that, because it's a long time since I've been sure whose side God is on. Since I was in those camps I've had to doubt his great goodness, in any case. On the other hand, I survived 'it' and simply can't deny the possibility that a miracle happened to me, the way I escaped the cannibals. You know, I can't believe in God and his laws any longer, but let's just say I don't want to forget him completely, either."

Of course I didn't say anything to Frau Kahn about my problem with the telephone plug, because she'd only laugh — she calls the Shabbat rules "only formalities, just silly," and a couple of times she's even told me, "Sometimes you just ought to do what you think is right and reasonable." Frau Kahn doesn't understand my fear, she doesn't understand that at home in Oran the fear of God was greater than was probably the case in Mannheim. "God be praised, honored, thanked" — those were no empty words, the way they are when they say them here. The whole day, the whole year was filled with words and things that you had to observe and fear, the magic numbers, the five fingers of your hand — you always had to see to it that "five" was mentioned in conversation — a number that had "five" as part of it. At the very least you had to say something like "So and so much plus five" when you were mentioning someone's age or the number of children: "How many children do you have?" "One plus five." That brought health and happiness. Don't touch this, don't walk past that, don't say that — rules, bits of advice, signs, numbers — we sought protection in such things. When we said goodbye, a glass of water was poured on the doorstep behind whoever was going away or on a trip, in order to insure a safe return, the same way the water of the ocean always comes back, but also so that the foot would remember that doorstep.

Once or twice a year we'd make a pilgrimage to the graves of the Holy Rabbis of Blessed Memory where we'd spend a few days praying and picnicking. A whole crowd of Arabs went along with us, because they had great respect for our holy rabbis, too, and trust in their miraculous powers; if they couldn't make the pilgrimage themselves, they sent their prayers for marriage, health, and business along with us. The Ashkenazim like Frau Kahn laugh about all that, they think we're superstitious and childish. Once I took Frau Kahn along to our synagogue, on Simchat Torah, when the men dance like crazy and call "Huwada!" in Arabic at the same time — "He will come!" (If only he'd just come soon!) "Huwada!" First they shout, then they yell and stamp their feet, while the women cheer and throw bonbons over the separating partition, scream and screech, "Youyouyou," clap their hands, and throw their arms out toward the Torah scrolls that the men are dancing with. Then we kiss our hands and cover our eyes before so much blinding light. He will come! Huwada!

Frau Kahn was completely horrified; she probably hadn't really understood earlier that we come from Arab countries. "Please don't hold it against me, but that's not for me," she said. "I don't want to go to your synagogue again — that's so foreign to me. No, no, that's not for me, really it's not."

The Ashkenazim are always so cool and controlled, I don't see how they can get through a day like Yom Kippur without fear and without tears, when God determines "who will live and who will die, who will perish by water, who by fire, who will die by violence, who from hunger, who from thirst, who will perish in storms or from the plague, who will be crushed or choked to death. To whom it will be granted to find rest and who will have to wander throughout the world, who will live in peace and who in times of destruction, who will live in joy and who in sorrow, who will be rich and who poor, and who will be humiliated and who exalted." You're already weak from fasting as it is and after a few hours you begin to get a headache, you're afraid and feel guilty and everything you've thought, said, and done has been seen through. No, then you just can't feel like you've been deserted by God, the way Frau Kahn sometimes says.

All my life I've accepted minor illnesses — or even slightly worse ones — and my misfortunes and weak moments as just punishment for neglect or even disobedience toward God; I've collected them, secretly added them together, and hoped that I've gotten the measure of misfortune and punishment that's my lot, so to speak, together in small sums. Every small and middle-sized loss was welcome to me. Every flu, every migraine, and every missed train or whatever halfway bad news gave me hope that maybe I'd be spared some really huge fright or loss and that maybe God wouldn't carry things too far with me — I really don't know why — because I love him, I fear him, and I don't reject him.

Frau Kahn and I didn't eat much on that Shabbat. I wanted her to take the rest of her fish and the dafina along, but she wouldn't. She said that was some sort of strange Sephardic custom, no thanks. So we cleared the table and I put the leftovers in plastic containers and stuck them in the deep freeze.

O N   T H E   F O U R T E E N T H   of July I've always gone to the military parade with the children, no matter what city we happened to be in. Ever since Zippora has had a girlfriend who lives on the Avenue de la Paix, she's wanted to go there, of course. She takes her sisters along and they can sit on the balcony quite comfortably and watch the parade from start to finish, while I have to find a place for me and the boys between people along the street, where I have to stand on tiptoe — even though, God knows, I'm tall — and give each of them a turn sitting on my shoulders, despite the fact that they've been too heavy for that for a long time.

"The military parade doesn't interest me at all . . . but the fireworks!" said Frau Kahn. "You've got to get out of the house, too, Frau Serfaty, you can't just fade away completely. You've already washed and cleaned and polished everything. So come on, today we're going to see the fireworks!"

I was frightened again, of course, that people would see me without my children and ask themselves, "What's she doing here all alone, where are the children?" But Frau Kahn would have none of that. "Simply sitting here waiting doesn't help either," she said, "and besides, it's dark and no one will see you anyway." She'd brought along a light blue beret and told me I should take off the kerchief and try on the cap; then she put it on me and tugged it around a little and said she thought I looked a lot better — not like someone you could tell was orthodox even from a distance. We left about half past nine, and in the crowds on the streets no one was paying much attention to anyone else, everyone was pushing and shoving, trying to get to the docks. Soon I even took off the beret, because it was much too hot. The street lights were turned off in order to make the fireworks stand out more brilliantly against the dark sky, and in several parts of the city they were already starting to crack and bang and blaze up simultaneously in all sorts of colors — flowers, stars, and golden rain that drifted down slowly. People yelled "Aah!" and "Ooh!" and clapped their hands and were excited — or at least not indifferent — and after each cascade of fire and every fiery flower, Frau Kahn looked at me from the side to see if I was yelling "Aah!" and "Ooh!" like everyone else and if I was having fun, and, yes, I was yelling "Aah!" and "Ooh!" just like everyone else and clapping, just as she expected me to.

After the fireworks the crowds got even worse than before, because now everyone started walking off in different directions and shoving and stumbling around and in some places people bunched up, then simply stopped where they were and blocked everything. Frau Kahn met several of her friends from the Cercle Vladimir Rabi and they said we should go and have something to drink at the outdoor café in front of the University until the crowd settled down — one of them was already sitting there to save some seats. Frau Kahn simply dragged me along. She was certainly happy that I'd put my cap back on in the meantime, so that I didn't look orthodox anymore, because the people from the Cercle Vladimir Rabi couldn't stand people who were orthodox.

At the café, everyone ordered cold drinks or ice cream and I ordered a "diabolo menthe." Frau Kahn and her friends talked about their last meeting, about the lecture they'd heard, "The Emancipation of the Jews and the French Revolution," and the discussion that followed. They went through the whole evening again — who said what and how this or that should be understood. At first I tried to listen to them, but since I really didn't belong to their group and hadn't been there that evening, and was, in other words, completely uninvolved, it seemed to me as if they'd taken their conversation off into an adjoining room and left me sitting all alone. And so my thoughts began to wander to my children again, of course. I still hadn't grasped what had actually happened. What if Simon had dragged the children off forever and I would only see them again as grownups, the girls as women and the boys as men, and perhaps they'd speak a foreign language and I'd have trouble recognizing them again and understanding them? I pictured them living like Marranos until that point, outwardly denying their love for their mother, but the older ones secretly telling the little ones about their mother again and again, to keep their memories alive, and those hidden, forbidden memories would give them hope of returning, something to hold them together. Until they came back, I'd have to arrange my life somehow; the best thing would probably be to move in with my sister, where I could certainly be of help with the kosher catering business, since they said they were getting more and more requests. I'd work during the day and take Billy out in the evening and walk through the gardens with him and talk to him about the children and in that way wait until years had gone by and the children had grown up. It would be easiest for them to find me at my sister's, and hopefully Billy, whom they loved so much, would still be alive.

I looked at the people in the outdoor café; they all looked so happy and lighthearted, as if they'd never had a care in their lives, but, of course, they were there to celebrate the fourteenth of July. In the meantime, one of Frau Kahn's friends had already ordered another round and I thought about how many years it had been since I'd just gone out for the evening and sat in an outdoor café without anyone hanging on me or yelling for me or accusing me or waiting for me. I had nothing to do and nothing to worry about. Suddenly, I thought about Oran, about our trips to the beach, when the whole family took off in the morning and camped out there between the city and the sea until late at night — the whole clan, all the uncles and aunts and the countless boy and girl cousins. There was cooking and eating and sleeping and we children played around between the blankets and the baskets from which new foods, fruits, sweets, and all sorts of goodies were constantly being pulled, as if they would never run out.

Since I arrived in Europe, all I've ever done is live inside, in cramped apartments and cramped streets, as if I were locked in some sort of chamber without an exit. Now I was happy to be sitting out under the sky, a wide, open, dark blue sky, in which there were still flashes and explosions, so that we all yelled "Ooh!" and "Aah!" The people around me were talking, smoking, and laughing; some had taken their shoes off and propped their bare feet on a chair, and I could still hear Frau Kahn talking with her friends, even arguing from time to time, and their voices got louder and louder, but I'd withdrawn, as if I were in an adjoining room, hearing them from a distance.

I ordered another diabolo menthe with a lot of ice and finally even smoked one of the cigarettes that a friend of Frau Kahn kept offering me. And so we stayed there until after midnight.

I SOMETIMES DREAM that I'm a prisoner. For days, years. I'm only free at night, for a few hours toward morning. During those hours I can walk around. But I don't know where to go. All the people I know are asleep, of course, and I'd frighten them if I were suddenly standing in front of their doors, sometime between night and morning. They haven't even seen me for years and are probably long since used to the idea that I've disappeared forever.

I carry my imprisonment through the streets of the city, and the boredom of imprisonment is behind me and in front of me as well, so what it amounts to is that I'm just as imprisoned in those hours of freedom as I am in my cell. The imprisonment is senseless and the nocturnal freedom is too. Sometimes it's even worse — it's torment and revulsion.

Earlier, in Oran, one of my uncles sometimes interpreted my dreams for me. He'd say, "Come, sit down here and try to remember. Remember everything you saw in the dream and tell me about it, slowly." He'd fall silent, thinking it over, and then he'd ask about this or that detail again. In the early years when we were still friends, Simon would interpret my dreams, too. But when I wanted to learn how to interpret them myself, he said, "No, that's something you have to study for a long time, and it's not something for women." Occasionally he even refused to interpret a dream, for example that awful nightmare with the animal, half-cat, half-rabbit, that was gnawing at my foot. I was unable to get it off before my foot was half eaten away. I even begged other people to help me, but, though they tried, nobody could free me from that animal that was burrowing into my flesh. Simon said, "No, I can't explain that to you."

Once, I picked up one of the children's notebooks that was lying around unused, because I'd accidentally bought one ruled in small squares instead of the required big ones, and started to write down my dreams. I even took a label, pasted it on the front of the notebook, and wrote "Zohara's Dreambook" on it. Simon saw it and said right out that it was senseless to write down dreams and that the whole business of constantly writing things down was senseless. "Are you perhaps thinking of writing a book?" he sneered, and then he opened the sermons of Solomon and read out loud, "There is no end to this making of books. Too much work with the head wears down the body." I'd be better off thinking about the right time to soak the chickpeas for the dafina. I told him that if I couldn't interpret my dreams, I could at least pay some attention to them and write them down and then maybe sometime later I'd understand them.

And now I was dreaming about my children. That they were with me again, but we were living in a northern country where it was always cold and where there was always snow on the ground and polar bears running around. We were forced to live there for some inexplicable reason, but had no idea how we were supposed to and didn't have a thing and couldn't find anything to protect us from the cold. It occurred to me that Simon had once said, "Snow — that means drought, hunger, death."

You always think that something terrible has to appear with thunder and lightning, but that idea is completely wrong. Terrible things actually sneak up on you looking quite harmless, hidden in among everyday affairs, so that you don't recognize them right away.

One morning shortly after eleven, Frau Kahn rang the doorbell — she was pale and looked distressed. She made me go over to her apartment and then we were standing in her living room and lying on the little table in front of her sofa was a letter in Simon's handwriting — I recognized it immediately, of course. "But why did he address this letter to me?" said Frau Kahn. "It was lying there in my mailbox; I just took it out, not suspecting a thing, and I thought to myself, 'Who could be writing me from Argentina?'" In the envelope was a postcard with a picture of a city that stretched off into the distance, with mountains on the horizon, and on the reverse side were a few lines from Simon, saying he was in Argentina with the children. He'd bought a house. "Bought?" asked Frau Kahn. There, in that house in Argentina, he was now living with the children — the children were very happy and he would not be coming back, probably would never come back again. It was a wonderful country, Argentina. In addition, he'd already notified the pertinent agencies that the child support payments would no longer be necessary.

I screamed and Frau Kahn howled. While she ran out to get her sedative drops, I threw myself on her sofa and tossed the pillows — that always lay there in such a pretty row, each in its own place, the blue one, the pink one, the light yellow one, and the green one — onto the floor. Frau Kahn sat down beside me and collected them and stacked them on her lap. "Argentina, my

God, Argentina, can you figure it out?" she said over and over and then we took her sedative drops — ten for her and twenty for me.

Then it was as if someone had taken a blindfold from my eyes — yes, now I understood. Actually, I'd understood for a long time. Simon was not just a ridiculous show-off, a swindler, and a fraud; I'd already told him so, right to his face, at the railroad station in Kehl, but then I still didn't know he was a criminal, too — although I should have been able to sense it — as brazen and unrestrained as can be. "A holy man gone crazy," said Frau Kahn, "Oh, what am I saying, simply a crook, a common crook. I'm really ashamed for him."

I picked up the envelope and the postcard from Argentina and tore them up. I tore them into a hundred tiny, little pieces and threw the little pieces into the air so that they drifted down like confetti at a child's birthday party; and then I announced to Frau Kahn, loud and clear, "Oh no, I'm not going to be ashamed anymore. I've been ashamed long enough and didn't want to know the truth. Never asked and never said a thing. But now I've finally realized that I've been taken in. Simply taken in by a swindler and a crook, fell for his act and his lies and his craziness — even tried to understand him. Now I'm going to go to court, for justice and my rights. I'm going to bring charges."

At the police station they just shrugged their shoulders — what was so unusual about a father going off on a trip with his children, that certainly wasn't against any law. And the lawyer, one of Frau Kahn's friends from the Cercle Vladimir Rabi wouldn't, or couldn't, understand either. I lost my temper and started to yell, "This is a man who cheats, steals, and kidnaps, don't you understand? You've got to look for him and arrest him!" Maybe I yelled too loudly, maybe I came out with a few curses in Arabic. In any case, he didn't even want to hear the story to the end and sent me away, telling me I should settle down first. Early that evening, around half past five, after Frau Kahn had urged me to do it, I called Rabbi Hagenau and an hour later I was sitting in his office. On the phone I'd told him it was an urgent case, an extremely urgent case.

"Oh dear, rights and justice are big words," he told me, "but you yourself know the righteous perish and the godless lead the good life. We know little about such affairs. Unfortunately I can't promise you anything. There are already enough people running around promising things we can only dream about and claiming to know everything about everything. Your husband is probably one of that type. Not simply a liar, daydreamer, or a crook — more likely one of God's holy fools who's hard to control. One who believes he has to exaggerate evil in order to save the world — a little, false Messiah, who's now made himself invisible."

He knew what he was talking about, because Simon had managed to quarrel with every rabbi in every city, with his know-it-all attitude and his habit of sticking his nose into everything. Probably even Rabbi Hagenau had already heard a good deal about him from his colleagues in other cities and from the gossip in their congregations, since he himself travels a good deal and meets a lot of them.

Rabbi Hagenau's suits are not as dark as Simon's and his beard is not as long — it's actually rather short. His study was more like a businessman's office, with a bunch of gadgets all around that rang and beeped the whole time — Minitel, computer, fax, and a copying machine on which he wanted to copy Simon's letter right away, but I told him I'd ripped it up, to which he remarked that that wasn't going to help anything, and I didn't know whether he meant the tearing up or the copying. The telephone rang fairly often and each time he answered in a different language — Hebrew, English, French, or Yiddish; he even ran out a couple times to tell his wife something or because someone was at the door, which made me rather nervous.

Rabbi Hagenau is the judge of the congregation. He's already decided many legal disputes, presided over a bunch of divorces, determined where the boundary of the Shabbat should extend around the city, and has the authority over kosher foods. He visits the food producers, observes, analyzes, inspects and eventually gives his kosher stamp if everything meets with his approval; and sometime each fall, he and a troop of young men make the rounds of several of the vintners in the area to supervise the production of kosher wine. It was Rabbi Hagenau, as well, who declared that the butcher shop in the rue des Arcades was no longer kosher. One day people showed up and hanging there in the display window was a handwritten announcement that the kashrut was no longer assured there and that certification of the butcher shop had been withdrawn by Rabbi Hagenau. No one knows what happened to the poor butcher.

Frau Kahn, who doesn't much care for rabbis as it is, always calls him Rabbi Haargenau, which means "Rabbi Hairsplitter." She likes rabbis even less if they come from out-of-the-way places in Poland and try to transform a liberal European congregation according to the limited ideas of their shtetl. "That kind of thing really gets me worked up — where are we living, anyway?" she says.

But I often call him for advice, especially before Pesach, about the difficult details of the Pesach table, about the stove, the oven, the sink, and to reassure myself about all the food that suddenly shows up from almost anywhere — from Switzerland, from America, from Israel — and then you never know which of the kosher stamps can be trusted and which ones can't. In earlier years, Simon decided all that by himself and the list of stamps he trusted was correspondingly small. In later years, however, he never bothered about such things anymore and so I started to get the advice I needed from Rabbi Hagenau.

For a whole year I attended his course every Tuesday evening at 8:30, at a time when Simon was hardly coming home any longer. In the course, we worked our way through the prayer book so we'd be able to find our way around in it better and know what we were praying, rather than simply rattling off something we didn't understand. Rabbi Hagenau explained about the time and place the prayers originated, their relationship to other texts, and we discussed their meaning. It was a course only for women and a storm of indignation broke out, naturally, when we got to the place during the morning prayer where the men say, "Praise be unto You, Eternal One, our God, that You did not create me a woman," and where the women say instead, ". . . that You created me in a way pleasing unto You."

Rabbi Hagenau was able to explain at length that it didn't mean any sort of ranking between men and women, but, quite the opposite, that everyone should accept the place God had designated for him or her, a place we hadn't chosen but hadn't deserved either, and that, as it was, women were closer to God in their relative perfection, which is why it said, ". . . pleasing unto You." For that reason, women had fewer commandments to fulfill than men, who had a long road to hoe on the way to God's pleasure by fulfilling all of the numerous precepts.

We didn't quite believe him at the time and bored away with our questions until he finally shrugged his shoulders and said, "Well, I don't know what more I can say about it."

After class, while we were standing around in the hallway looking for the men, we decided that the evening had ended in a one-to-one tie: he hadn't convinced us, but we hadn't gotten him off the usual path, either.

Back then, Rabbi Hagenau had already asked me about Simon, who he was, how he came to call himself "Rabbi" and where he had acquired the title. I repeated what Simon had explained to me: from Singapore, that he was the Rabbi of Singapore. Then Rabbi Hagenau laughed just as loudly as Frau Kahn did when she heard it. "The Rabbi of where? Again, please?" "Of Singapore." He questioned me further about his studies, but I didn't know much about that. I told him about the Zohar and the book of Daniel, which Simon claimed to have studied so intensively. "The very books that no one understands," countered Rabbi Hagenau and shook his head. Of course I never told Simon a thing about the questioning, since I knew that he was already enraged at his "colleagues," who refused to recognize him and would only send him around the world to collect money. Later, I stopped going to the classes on Tuesday evenings because I was just too tired to go out again at half past eight in the evening.

And so, now I was sitting in Rabbi Hagenau's office, telling him everything that had happened, about the abduction of my children and, since I was already on the subject, about my whole messed-up life with Simon. How I'd married him without really knowing him, just out of loneliness and fear of never having children. How he dragged me and the children from one city to another, where we never really settled down, but always had our bags half packed, ready to leave again. And how he became more and more pious — if you can even call it piety — and was always either completely silent or screaming, always knowing better, smashing up tables and throwing them in the trash and calling himself the Rabbi of Singapore and claiming to collect money for holy purposes but was, in reality, stealing. How he lived together with us at first, but then was only a visitor and eventually a stranger who acted like a big deal in front of us when he did show up, and how he finally made off with the children. And that I couldn't see any sense to his having done it, other than evil, evil unto itself — just to humiliate me, hurt me, destroy me. But for what reason? And maybe he wasn't really crazy at all, but, instead, a completely cold-blooded criminal who had his own plans. Maybe he wanted to start a kosher Mafia in Argentina and train the children to be a gang of swindlers and false rabbis, in order to be able to send them out into the world again as disciples and proclaimers of his greed. In any case, I had to get the children back again, whatever it cost, and now I was demanding my rights and justice.

Rabbi Hagenau listened to it all and then said, "We need to be modest, you understand — first we need to find a modest, practical solution, a reasonable one. First things first. First the children and then justice and righteousness." But he was rather excited as he said that, constantly clicking his ballpoint pen — in, out, in, out. "We have to lure him into a trap, figure out a trick, perhaps even walk a crooked path — reason often follows crooked paths." Was I ready for that? I answered that I understood very well that we had to act and that I was ready for anything. "We'll get them back for sure," he said. "We'll cast a net in which he'll get tangled up and then we'll take the children away from him. You know of course, Mrs. Serfaty, that rabbis all over the world know each other somehow. I'll call three or four of them in other cities and they'll call three or four others in other cities; and besides that there are the rabbinical conferences where you meet each other and all the Bar Mitzvahs and wedding ceremonies where we see each other again, and our children have married into families in all different countries, so the net is actually already cast. We could call it the 'Torah connection.'" He couldn't stop laughing over the joke. "If your husband is still putting on such pious airs, sooner or later he'll run across some rabbi or other, best of all in North America or Europe, and then he'll walk into the trap, irresistible — snap! and it's closed." He slapped the top of the table so hard with the flat of his hand that the gadgets jumped. One of the telephones started to ring right away, but everything had been said already. His wife accompanied me to the door and we spoke a few words to one another and although she couldn't really understand at all, I told her I probably would have done better to have simply taken the children and left long ago. But where would we have gone?

I HAD PUT ASIDE my fears and my shame and taken the kerchief off my head as well. Most of the time, now, I'd leave the house around ten o'clock and a quarter of an hour later I'd have crossed the boundary of my territory and entered foreign territory, even though there was nothing I needed to get or do there. I simply walked around without reason or destination, into the city, along streets, wherever they led me, stopped in front of the show windows and took a good, long look at the displays that I'd just rushed by for years, and whenever I strolled along that way without purpose and allowed myself time for totally useless things, I felt something like courage rising within me, or at least some sort of relief, and was no longer afraid.

The days were still long and the summer still so hot, but here it's not the same heat as it was in Oran, where a slight breeze blew in constantly from the sea and where we had tiled floors onto which we threw a bucket of water every so often; no, it's the humid heat of the plains between the mountain ranges that I find so hard to bear.

I had nothing to do, didn't even have to think about getting lunch, didn't have to decide whether I should make couscous with vegetables or noodles with tomato sauce, or whether I'd just take some sausages out of the freezer and stick them in a half a baguette with some lettuce — the children call that a "hamburger." They're already yelling, as soon as they come through the door, that they're hungry and one doesn't want vegetables and the other doesn't want noodles, but we really can't eat "hamburger" every day — the only thing they can always agree on.

I bought myself a piece of cake at the baker's and ate it on the street, like I did after school with my friends in Amiens — secretly, of course, because my mother would never have permitted me to buy a piece of cake from a goyish baker and, of course, my children weren't allowed to, either.

Once I walked down a broad avenue and then kept going through all sorts of streets leading in the direction of the old city where I'd never set foot in all those years. In most of the houses, the windows were wide open and I could hear the sound of plates and silverware being banged together and chairs being pulled up to the table and this time it seemed to me that now the others were prisoners within their homes and habits, while I could walk around freely and live however the mood struck me.

The city seemed to be fairly empty on the outskirts, but toward its center it gradually filled up with people — singly, in pairs, families, large and small groups. I walked past the docks and around the old city; moving by out on the water were steamers and excursion boats, from which snatches of foreign languages were carried over by the breeze; children waved from deck — they were probably bored and not interested in the tour guide's narration. And I walked around like someone who was taking a vacation in her hometown, in the midst of people who came from foreign countries to sightsee, and it was almost as if I were discovering a new continent, another America, and those people running around in front of me were the natives, half naked and adorned with hats, kerchiefs, and cameras. I studied them and laughed at them.

Suddenly the idea struck me that I should go to the hairdresser, but for that I returned to my own familiar territory, to Coiffure Gerard at our corner, a shop that I walk by every day but had never gone into. Only once in my life did I ever have my hair done and that was before my marriage to Simon. The hairdresser was one of my mother's acquaintances from Algeria who'd opened a hairdressing and cosmetic salon. Her name was Madame Ayache and I didn't go to her but, instead, she came to our house on the day before the wedding, set my hair and gave me a manicure, because my nails were in pretty sad shape from working in the hospital. Then she painted my hands with henna, in a fine pattern that looked as if I were wearing lace gloves. The women and girls of the family stood all around me, then they all got their hands painted, too. How many times I took part in such festivities as a child! Only the sisters, cousins, and close friends of the bride were painted; then they were full of themselves and ran around for days with the designs on their hands — proud, because it was a sign that once again someone from the family had stood under the chuppah. Getting married was really the most important thing of all.

For the wedding I borrowed a wig and, later, always wore a kerchief. In the morning I simply slipped it over my head without even looking in the mirror. It was considered very commendable for us women if we fulfilled the obligation to cover our hair. Simon paid close attention to make sure that right

after I got up, or later in the morning, I didn't go running
around with my hair showing, and told the story over and over
about the woman whose sons had all become great scholars and
holy men of our people: that was her reward for the fact that
not even the walls of their house had ever seen her hair.

At Coiffure Gerard I asked for a wash and set. The hairdresser
suggested a lot of different cuts and I chose the one that seemed
least conspicuous to me. Then she combed, brushed, poked, cut,
pulled, and twisted my hair, and I sat opposite my reflection in
the mirror and had no idea when the last time was that I looked
at myself for so long in the mirror. I looked, and had to ask
myself what had really become of me. It seemed to me that I had
never come to my senses since the day I stood on the ship with
my mother and sister and looked back at Oran. Our mother had
said to us, "Say farewell — you'll never come back to this place
again." And she cried, as did everyone else on the ship. The
smaller the silhouette of the city became, the more it sank away
and disappeared, the louder the crying and lamenting became
until everyone went below deck, as if into their own coffins,
when nothing more was to be seen but a gray sky and a gray sea
that no longer had a coast.

Rabbi Hagenau or his wife must have passed on what happened, because now the telephone never stopped ringing —
the mothers of my children's friends called and said they'd heard
about it, it was absolutely unbelievable, how awful, how horrible, what a monster he was, and they asked whether they could
do anything for me, help out some way, do the shopping, take
care of anything, or whether I needed anything at all. Soon a
few actually came to my door, rang the bell, rushed right in and
sat down in the living room — they wanted to hear all the
details and then told about all sorts of other terrible things that
had happened and misfortunes they'd heard about in other

places, at other times. Suddenly I was nearly deluged by friendship or friendliness or, at least, something that seemed like it. In that short time I got to know people, more and more people, after all the years in which I'd hardly ever spoken to a single person in that city, just as I hadn't in all the other cities that had come before. My new acquaintances invited me to their houses, I sat at their tables, and of course I'd already seen all of them somewhere or other — in the synagogue, at parents' meetings, or when I met the children after kindergarten; we'd said hello a thousand times already, *how are you, hope things are going well, good, thanks.* You always say you're fine, because in reality you remain quite distant from each other, and you can't just say, "Things are terrible. If you only knew how bad I feel today."

A sort of kinship grew up around my misfortunes, mostly out of sympathy, naturally, but also from the excitement over this unusual event and gratitude that it hadn't happened to them. I certainly understood that, but still; all the good it did me to feel that now I was the center of interest rather than always being on the outside. But then when I was sitting at the table with my new friends, they no longer asked about my children and my husband — whom they'd just finished calling a monster — as if they were afraid that something terrible could get into their houses, too. There was dafina and tahini, just like in Oran; they tried to persuade me to eat more and then even more, just like in Oran, and afterwards gave me food in plastic containers and cake in bags, and that was really exactly like in Oran. We said nothing more about my misfortune, at least not at the table with everyone there, but only when I was leaving, already in the doorway, whispering, alone with the woman whose home it was.

EVER SINCE I'd liberated myself from shame and my unworthy life, I felt more and more certain that now the liberation of my children couldn't be much farther off either, with God's help. I became calm, the way I'd been in the days right before I brought the children into the world, when I eventually felt clearly, with each one, that the time had come. It was that way even with Michael, who came three weeks early; the doctor and the midwife wanted to send me home from the hospital, said it was still much too early, not to even think about delivery, but I stayed and told them, "It's time, I know it is."

Rabbi Hagenau called almost every day. He said the net had been cast, that he'd called all around and sent letters to the four corners of the earth. Several of his colleagues hadn't wanted to hear a thing about the whole business and had said, "But we're not the police," or "Problems like that between husband and wife are ticklish, they're hard to understand." But others had listened to everything and even made more telephone calls themselves and had asked around and written letters; they'd even met with some success already — they were on his trail. Simon appeared to have left Argentina some time ago and was said to have shown up in London. "London — that's already much, much simpler," said Rabbi Hagenau. "Be ready to go, Mrs. Serfaty, pack a small bag."

And so I put a little suitcase beside the door, all ready to grab, just as in the last weeks of my pregnancies. I was no longer just waiting for my children, I was already expecting them.

Among the advertisements that were always lying in the mailbox, I found one for a sale on paints and painting equipment. I went to the building supply center that was mentioned and bought two rolls of burlap wallpaper and two buckets of white paint with a touch of yellow, a roller, and a brush for the corners. If the children were going to return, they weren't coming back to the same tired, old children's room, but to one that was freshly painted for a new beginning — everything was going to be completely different. I pushed the seven beds, the night tables and chests into the middle of the room and tore off the old paper, the one with the little butterflies, having failed, in the end, to solve the problem of whether there were more butterflies with spots or without them.

The next morning I got up on the ladder and painted the ceiling and by evening had already started to paper. Around six Frau Kahn came over. She didn't look well; she had to hold onto the ladder because she was so dizzy and I almost fell off because the ladder wobbled so much. I convinced her to call Dr. Schwab, who actually came fairly quickly and sent her to the hospital. "That's really safer," he said. We called a taxi and I went with her, and on the way Frau Kahn said that she'd been so depressed recently that she hardly felt like living anymore. I tried to convince her that it would soon pass, that it was because of the heat we were all suffering from — all we needed was a good thunderstorm. But she said, "No, it's my heart, it's worn out." She asked me to call her son, who was vacationing in Switzerland at the time — maybe he'd come and see her. "You know, I'm his mother, I can't come right out and ask him."

When she heard that Raffael was going to come, Frau Kahn perked right up and felt hopeful again, even for me, too. "You'll see, Frau Serfaty," she said, "we'll soon be together with all of our children again."

The paint dried quickly with the heat, but, despite it, you could see that the summer was gradually coming to an end. The people from the building were coming back from vacation one by one and even at the market I soon saw the old faces again.

And then — it was Wednesday afternoon, *One for All* was on the television and I was standing on the ladder, painting the part of the wall above the curtain rod, when the telephone rang and Rabbi Hagenau said, "This is it. You must come over immediately, with your suitcase. Immediately."

It usually takes a quarter of an hour to get to Rue Ehrmann, but this time I made it in five minutes. I grabbed the packed bag beside the door and quickly dropped off the apartment key with Raffael, who yelled after me that he was going to be able to bring his mother home from the hospital today, and I yelled back over my shoulder, "That makes it even better, thank God!" When I arrived, Rabbi Hagenau was already sitting in his car with the motor running; I got in beside him and we were off. "I'm taking you to the airport now," he said. "You're catching the flight to London. The plane leaves at 4:20. If all goes according to plan, you could be back by midnight and perhaps you won't even need your bag." He handed me two envelopes, a fat one and a thin one. In one was a single ticket and in the other there were six.

Only then did he tell me how Simon had fallen into the trap — he'd just heard it on the phone from his colleague in London. It turned out that Simon had left the children in the care of a woman in Stamford Hill, where the Chassidim live, while he was working his swindles in other parts of the city — as they'd now found out. The woman couldn't help noticing that the children were all wearing brand-new things, all with the label of the same Argentine firm, that there was no sign of a mother, and that the children wouldn't answer any of her questions, no matter what language she tried, especially when she asked where their mother was. In the evenings they were picked up by their father and no one knew where they all disappeared to. The woman got suspicious and told her husband everything; they talked it over and notified their rabbi, who in turn called Rabbi Hagenau several times and got more details about Simon. They could deal at length with the "Rabbi of Singapore," he'd said, when the children were once again with their mother. And Simon was not going to get off lightly, Rabbi Hagenau added, because all the money he'd collected over the years for good causes had gone into his own pocket and he'd now started to swindle his former countrymen, the Moroccan Arabs. In the back rooms of their shops he was palming himself off as a miracle worker, and, of course, demanding payment in advance for the miracle, after which he'd disappear for good. The Arabs from Morocco trusted him because he looked like a rabbi and because he came from Marrakesh, and no matter what happened, no Marrakeshi was ever going to report another Marrakeshi to the European police.

We went roaring down the highway and Rabbi Hagenau gave the impression of being very nervous. He drove like a lunatic, honking the horn, passing, constantly changing lanes and forcing the cars ahead of us to get out of the way, all the while lecturing me to keep calm, that's what mattered above all in this situation, a cool head was the most important thing, the plan to kidnap the children back had been worked out perfectly, all the people involved were standing by at their posts, just waiting for the signal to be given — everything, absolutely everything, from here on depended on me, I'd have to turn into a kind of James Bond, as it were, just for a day, if that was possible for me to do.

In truth I was quite calm — in any case, calmer than Rabbi Hagenau imagined; I was, after all, completely certain of my cause. Certain that I was in the right, certain that my children would soon be with me again and certain that now a different life would begin, one without illusions, because I'd believed much too long in reconciliation and a happy ending.

In the beginning, when I first got to know Simon, I was grateful to him for relieving my loneliness; that gratitude had lasted a long time and almost became a form of subjugation. And so, against my will, I became an accessory to his shady existence and, as a result, almost a sort of accomplice. Because he realized that I rejected that life, he eventually turned away from me entirely, abandoned the children, and got more and more caught up in his swindles and fantasies, until the day he took his revenge because I didn't want to be his accomplice and had laughed at his delusions.

Around ten to four we arrived at the airport at Entzheim; Rabbi Hagenau steered me through the crowds of people to the right counter, all the while emphasizing that a Chassid from Stamford Hill would meet me at the airport in London and take me to the proper place, while the local rabbi lured Simon away and kept him busy with some excuse or other, some made-up big deal that Simon wouldn't be able to resist.

I'd never traveled on an airplane before; the only big trip I'd ever taken was the crossing by ship from Oran. Later there were no more trips, just moving from one city to another, chasing around after Simon's delusions in a borrowed pickup truck into which were crammed a few suitcases, a few pieces of furniture, his sacred books, and one more child each time. Otherwise the only trips were on the train to visit my sister in the suburbs of Paris.

I may have given the impression that I didn't quite know what to do when I got into the airplane, in contrast to the group of young girls who sat down next to me and to whom everything seemed routine; they took piles of newspapers from the little table at the entrance right away and it seemed like they were laughing at me. The airplane wasn't much larger than a bus and we were the only passengers. I took my little prayer book out of the travel kit I'd kept ready and looked for the "Prayer for Travelers" located among the blessings for various occasions. "May it be pleasing unto You, O Eternal One, our God and God of our fathers, to accompany us in peace and to let us journey in peace and arrive at our destination in peace and joy, and to permit us to return home again in peace. Protect us from misfortune and accident and rescue us if we are waylaid or fall into the hands of enemies. Hear our prayer and let us find mercy and compassion in Your eyes. Praise be unto You, Eternal One, our God, You who hears our prayers."

The airplane shook all over and sometimes it seemed to drop suddenly and the girls squealed while I prayed. Then the stewardess came down the aisle balancing the supper trays; I got one that was all wrapped up and sealed, which Rabbi Hagenau had obviously ordered especially for me; his certificates with the stamps and signatures were impossible to miss, pasted across the package in several places.

Slowly the shaking and lurching calmed down and when I looked out of the window, the countryside beneath us was quite flat; "Belgium," the stewardess said. And then I saw the sea and the coast of England, exactly as it was on the map of the weather forecast. I'd just been standing on the ladder in my apartment, having problems with the part of the wall above the curtain rod where it's so hard to paint, and on television — as it does every day at that time — *One for All* was playing; and now, after exactly one hour had passed, there I was, sitting in an airplane, flying across Europe. Something compelled me to keep thinking about the renovations I'd begun, what was going to happen to the buckets and paint brushes, the ladder, and all the mess and if, maybe, after Raffael had picked up his mother at the hospital, he'd be able to finish the renovations and put the things away in the cellar. I couldn't think about anything else.

The London airport must be located on an island — all I saw was water to the right and left of the runway, but I told myself that water was less dangerous than the mountains and there wasn't going to be an airplane crash now because my collection of misfortunes was already complete, there couldn't be any reason to add to it. We landed without a problem, had to walk down the steps and across the apron to a big, new building, then through the corridors and up escalators, and on both sides were all those advertisements and showcases and notices in a language I couldn't understand a bit — English. It was not only that I couldn't understand what was written there, but that everything looked different: the colors, the shape of the lettering, even the little, individual details — the doors and latches, the windows and light switches, all the things that you hardly notice otherwise. I got pretty anxious and my self-assurance began to wobble; actually, it almost collapsed under those foreign impressions in a place where I'd never set foot, where there were no familiar sights, no familiar sounds, and not even a familiar smell. But in the arrival area, there actually was a Chassid standing there with a sign in his hand, which said "ZOHARA" in big letters, and at the sight of him I calmed down again. The sign wouldn't have been necessary, because there weren't many Chassidim standing there, and even though I'd never met a Chassid in my life, I ran over to him as if he were a close relative, and he was already starting toward me as well. Of course we didn't shake hands.

From then on it was one thing after another: I walked, I ran, and I rode beside my Chassid, and I no longer knew whether to be reassured or depressed. Right after he introduced himself — "My name is Mordechai" — we started to run. We ran down stairs, up stairs, crossed a couple of streets, tore into an underground garage, ran around between the cars until I thought we'd finally ended up at the right one, but we had to run off in a different direction until we finally did get to it. Mordechai, the Chassid, drove a Volvo like most of the Jews in England, maybe as a delayed tribute to Raoul Wallenberg and the King of Sweden who had sent him. Frau Kahn told me the story; they'd once had an evening memorial program for Wallenberg at the Cercle Vladimir Rabi. In the car, the Chassid started to speak English to me and when I said, "No. No English," he asked, "Yiddish?" Where was I supposed to have learned Yiddish? I asked back, "Arabic?" And he just answered "Chas veshalom" — "God help us" in Hebrew.

It was the first time in my life that I'd met a Jew with whom I had no common language, so all that was left to try to understand each other somehow was Hebrew, of which I knew at least some words and expressions from the prayers, blessings, and the Haggadah, because I had, after all, worked through the weekly lessons of the Torah for years with my uncle back in Oran. I said, "Gam zu l'tova," or "Even that will be to the good," an expres-

sion that almost always fits and the Chassid answered, "Chazak!"
— "Bravo!"

We'd been driving through the city for a long time when I
finally asked him, "Ayei yeladim?" — "Where are the children?"
The Chassid pointed up front, beyond the houses, and said,
"Makom habah" — "At that place," Stamford Hill, and then I
soon began to see more and more, then nothing but black-suited
men with ringlets on their temples, sometimes discretely pulled
back over their ears, and women with wigs and loads of children
sitting in or hanging on or running around baby carriages with
rows of seats. Then the Chassid stopped in front of a house and
indicated that he was going to pray Minchah, but would be back
in a few minutes. Before that, he put on a cassette with Chassidic
songs, and out came "Moshiach, Moshiach," but I wanted to
hear about my children rather than about Moshiach, so I pressed
Pause. Then the Chassid came running out of the house again
— obviously he'd just gotten an important message. We roared
off in the car and stopped only a few blocks further on, in front
of a house that looked exactly like all the others. There he
pushed me out of the car and said, "Lech!" and, as if to say it
more emphatically, "Lech lecha!" just the way God said to Abraham, "Go into the land . . ." — it's right in the second or third
weekly lesson. After I'd gotten out, he yelled after me, "Kachta
yeladim!" — "Get the children!" In front of the door of the
house stood a woman in a wig who motioned me in, then
pulled and dragged me up the steps without saying a word; up-
stairs she pushed open a door and behind that door sat my children, one beside the other, just like they did in Dr. Schwab's
waiting room, each one clutching a bag from Marks & Spencer.
We all screamed at the same time and wanted to throw our arms
around each other and cry, but the unknown woman in the wig

shoved us all out of the room and down the stairs again, out of the house, and through the garden. The Chassid had already opened all four doors of the car and yelled, "Yetsiat England!" We piled into the car, the woman pushed the doors shut from the outside and waved while the Chassid started up, and we sped away as if Pharaoh were actually pursuing us with his army. I sat beside the Chassid, the children were packed together in the back, and I had to turn around to hold their hands and caress them; little Jonathan hung on my neck so that I almost choked, Ruth hung on Jonathan, and they were all talking and screaming at once and pulling candy out of their Marks & Spencer bags at the same time and, of course, I couldn't understand anything they were saying. In the rear window behind them I could see how the city was receding further and further and I thought the Chassid was right, this was our exodus from Egypt, even if the Sinai was still far away and the entire desert was still to be crossed. The Chassid turned on his tape again and each time it came out with "Moshiach" he sang along in a loud voice, which got louder and louder until we arrived at the airport. Then I took the pack of tickets from my bag, towed the line of children up to the Air France counter where we said goodbye to Mordechai, the Chassid, who sent us off with a torrent of blessings: that God might be merciful and benevolent to us and watch over our going out and coming in and grant a life in peace and comfort to us and to our whole family, but before he got to "all Israel" we had to leave him standing there so we wouldn't miss our plane.

In the airplane we didn't know how to sit in order to be as close to each other as possible; later I took Ruth and Jonathan on my lap and Michael and Daniel sat beside us. Zippora and Elisheva acted like they were too cool for all that and sat down behind us, after whispering to me that they were sick and tired of playing mother and had done enough flying in airplanes, too.

When we arrived at Strasbourg at half-past ten, Rabbi Hagenau was at the airport again to pick us up. The closer we came to the city and our house, the quieter my children became, and by the time we walked into our building and our apartment, they were absolutely silent. In the living room a little group was waiting for us — my sister and Elias, Frau Kahn and her son Raffael. My sister and Elias had even prepared a buffet supper for us — it's their specialty, after all. But then we stood around quite stiffly, like people who weren't acquainted with each other, who didn't have anything to say and were embarrassed; little Jonathan started to cry and Ruth didn't even go "ssh!" to him a single time. That lasted until the dog finally came out from under the table, after he'd figured out who'd come in the door — not some new guests from whom you had to hide even further under the table, but his old friends from summer vacations. He jumped all over the children for joy, and then they seemed to have been released from their trance and yelled "Billy, oh Billy, our Billy!" and took him into their room and played on the beds.

There was always something curious about the dog: the more the children loved him, the more Simon hated him. He hated the sight of him and, as a matter of fact, all animals frightened him. Once, at Purim, when the children turned up in animal masks and costumes that they'd put together in kindergarten and at school, he jumped and shook so much it was as if real lions and wild animals had forced their way into our apartment. He tore off their masks and screamed, while we laughed and yelled that they were only costumes, it was only for Purim.

Then the guests in the living room finally turned their attention to the cold buffet. Elias uncorked the champagne "in honor of the day," Rabbi Hagenau gave the blessing, and everyone called out "L'chayim!" and clinked their glasses, while I stood in the hallway, outside, between the rooms, half looking

at the children and half listening to the guests. My sister was saying that she and our mother had never really trusted Simon —
he'd been much too pious to be normal — and Frau Kahn told
the story of the "Rabbi of Singapore" again and everyone had
a good laugh.

But then they probably noticed that I wasn't really in the
mood for laughing and I told them I was tired and that my back
hurt. Rabbi Hagenau was the first to leave, and then Raffael,
who quickly gathered up the last of the painting things that were
still lying around. For my sister and Elias, I made up the former
marriage bed in our former bedroom; we simply took the junk
off the bed and threw it down wherever there was still space.

I went across to the children who were busily taking over
their room again. Daniel and Michael had already pulled out all
their Mickey Mouse and Asterix comic books and laid them
out on their beds and were starting to read. Zippora and Elisheva put the whole parade of their favorite actors and singers
up on the wall again; absolutely no one had noticed the renovations. But Jonathan and Ruth, who'd already undressed and
were crawling around under the beds in their Argentine underwear, discovered the ship made of Lego blocks and asked me,
"Did you build that?" and I answered, "Yes, I built that." Zippora and Elisheva said they still had a whole bunch of things to
tell me, but not now, not in front of the little ones, and I, too,
said, "No, not now, it's much too late for that today, almost two
o'clock in the morning, now we really ought to go to bed, and
the day after tomorrow is the first day of school already."

Frau Kahn had waited for me in the living room. She wanted
to help me clean up, but I told her that it could very well wait
until tomorrow. I was happy that she was feeling better again.
She'd even put on lipstick and that was a good sign. Afterward
we stood outside by the elevator for another few minutes and

talked, just as we had a few weeks before, about everything that had happened and Frau Kahn said, "Now you really need to have a good rest, Frau Serfaty, and take a lot of vitamin C." Then we each said, "Good night" and "Until tomorrow" and closed our apartment doors.

I sat down in the living room for a few minutes and finally ate a couple of the little pizzas from the buffet and drank a glass of champagne, too. Then I stretched out in the easy chair the way I usually do on the Shabbat and probably fell asleep, because toward morning there was little Jonathan suddenly standing in front of me, saying, "Mama, come to bed!"

ABOUT THE AUTHOR

Barbara Honigmann was born in 1949 in East Berlin, where her parents had returned after the war. She works as a dramatic advisor and theater producer, and has lived in Strasbourg, France, since 1984. She has published several novels. In 1994 she received the Nicolas Born Award, and in 2000 she was awarded the prestigious Kleist Prize, given to promising, young artists.

ABOUT THE TRANSLATOR

John Barrett worked for many years as a cardiologist before turning to translation with Grete Weil's *The Bride Price*, which was named an Outstanding Translation of the Year by the American Literary Translators Association. He lives in New Hampshire.

A LOVE MADE OUT OF NOTHING
& ZOHARA'S JOURNEY

was set in Bembo, a typeface based on the types used by the
Venetian scholar-publisher Aldus Manutius in the printing of
De Ætna, written by Pietro Bembo and published in 1495.
The original characters were cut in 1490 by Francesco Griffo,
who at Aldus's request later cut the first italic types. Originally
adapted by the English Monotype Company, Bembo is one
of the most elegant, readable, and widely used
of all old-style book faces.

Design by Stefan Betz Bloom